A Co

a novel

Johnny Saghani

SALMON RUN PRESS

Anchorage   London   Sydney   Moscow

A COLD DAY TO DIE

Copyright © 1998 Johnny Saghani

ISBN 1-887573-04-6

All rights reserved. No portion of this manuscript may be reproduced by any means, either mechanical or electronic, without express permission by the author or publisher except in the case of brief quotations embodied in critical articles and reviews. Address all inquiries to: Salmon Run Press, P. O. Box 672130, Chugiak, AK 99567-2130.

The author would like to thank Michael Dorris, National Book Critics Circle Award-winner, for editing half of this manuscript. Michael died in April 1997 before the novel was completed. The author would also like to thank the following people for editing parts of the original manuscript: Rod Clark, Teresa Scott, & P. S.

This book is a work of fiction. Names, characters, places, quotes, and incidents are used fictitiously. Any resemblance to actual events or locales or persons, living or dead, is coincidental.

10 9 8 7 6 5 4 3 2

"An extraordinary story on an extreme landscape. This is a minor classic."

— *Philadelphia Herald*

"A stunning and powerful first novel."

— *New York Star Tribune*

"*A Cold Day to Die* is as good as it gets."

— *Chicago Newsday*

"Among the most brilliant younger writers in recent American literature."

— *Allen Ginsberg*

"An exceptional first novel— masterful and moving, real and remarkable."

— *Calgary Telegraph*

"Poignant and true. A first rate novel about a Native American man without hope, caught in the collision of two worlds."

— *International Booklist Review*

"Having tricked the village men into gathering beneath the steep mountain, Raven flew to the top and jumped up and down on a great overhang of heavy snow. He jumped and jumped until it avalanched down upon those Indians, burying them. Raven waited until spring and then he ate them all, pecking out their eyes first."

Chapter 1

After the traffic light finally turned red, Philip Highmountain crossed the busy intersection. Both up and down the city street the Indian could see other people walking on the sidewalks and in and out of storefronts. Two women staggered out from a bar, holding onto two each other's arms for support. Philip knew they were whores. The women were both Native and they had short legs and baggy jeans held up by wide leather belts. They smelled of beer when they passed, laughing as they turned and walked away from Highmountain and into another bar only two doors away.

Many village girls came to the cities looking for opportunities. Broke and dissolutioned, they usually ended up on the streets. Half of the drunks downtown were from villages. Men and women alike came in search of jobs. The unfortunate ones wound up here.

In the summer, tourists lined the streets with

expensive cameras strung around their necks. They went in and out of tourist shops and returned home with authentic Native souvenirs which they showed on their walls and shelves with pride. For years to follow, they would brag about their high-priced Native art, never once thinking about the people who made them. Then the city was spit-polished for tourists. Every window was washed, and beautiful and fragrant flowers were hung along the clean-swept avenues. Giftshops invited customers inside with colorful signs, promises of low prices, and fresh-brewed coffee. Everything was tended to except for the hungry Indians, whose hands and backs were strong. A century before they would have hunted on this land and fished shimmering salmon from the frigid waters beyond. They would have raised families, become elders and grandparents, and they would have died one day with many kin to remember their meaningful and hard-lived lives.

    Now it was early winter and the tourists were gone, and in the gray light of day downtown looked like the residue of a party or a great and splendid parade the morning after. The city was cold, and a northern wind swept down from the mountains straight through the heart of the city, blowing garbage against curbs and piling snowdrifts against the tires of parked cars. The sharp edge of wind passed through Philip Highmountain's flesh like a knife and buried deep within his bones. He turned up his collar and stood on the far side of the street, watching people passing and cars beginning to move again now that the traffic light had turned green.

Nearby, a short Indian man was talking to a woman. Highmountain could hear that the man was trying to sell her a piece of ivory which his father had carved back in their village. It might have sold quickly in the summer to toursists and rich foreigners, but now there would be only the hard-sell. After the woman left, shaking her head, the man turned and started toward Highmountain until he saw that he was Indian too. But that wasn't all that made him stop. There was something that frightened him in Highmountain's face. It wasn't a hateful or angry quality, but something hardened and dangerous. The peddlar could sense that this was a man who was used to confined spaces and uncomfortable with the openess of the streets. The deadness in the man's eyes repelled him and he walked quickly away uptown, looking for a less threatening customer. Someone with money.

Highmountain took one last pull from his cigarette and threw it to the ground. It was his last one. For a moment he watched its thin wisp of smoke blown frantic by the wind, never holding one direction for long. Like the garbage and drifts, it was held captive by the wind. The Indian saw too much of himself in his tossed cigarette, and he crushed it hard beneath his boot before descending the stairs which led into the bar.

It was dark and warm inside. Philip looked around. It was still early in the afternoon and there weren't many people sitting at the tables or at the bar. He hadn't been inside the place for several years. Not much had changed, though. There was a new mirror behind the bartender, and he didn't recognize some of the neon lights advertising beer brands. He ordered what was on tap and listened to the music. Philip recognized two Native men sitting at a small booth.

One of them waived at him, motioning him to come over.

Philip took his draft and walked over to where they sat.

"Hey, Highmountain!" exclaimed the shorter man, who faltered as he tried to stand up, but steadied himself before he almost fell back down.

The man wore a blue T-shirt with a big yellow smiley face on the front.

"What are you doing here, man? Did they let you out of the joint already?" he asked while the other man listened, nursing his drink and cigarette.

Philip took a long drink from his glass until it was nearly empty before speaking to the man.

"Just got out this morning," he said while setting the glass on the dark wood table beside an ashtray filled with butts and ash.

"How long were you in for this time?" asked the short man.

Highmountain didn't answer right away. He looked around until he saw the mirror behind the bar. He stared at his reflection. In it he could see the short man reach for his arm.

"Hey, Phil. This is my friend Johnny Kasnoff. He's part Indian. I guess he's real Indian all right. So, come on man, what'd they get you for?"

The man named Johnny reached for his pack of Camels and knocked over his beer, spilling it all over the table. It dripped off the edge onto his leg.

Highmountain took a cigarette from the pack on the table, lit it, and exhaled slowly before speaking again.

"Assault," he whispered, leaning over the table.

"Sit down. Here, have another beer," said the short man.

"Yea. Sure, Joe," the Indian replied, sitting down beside him.

"Bartender! Another draft!" Philip yelled across the room, waving his hand.

"Shit, Philip. You're always in trouble," said Joe, who was from a small village upriver from where Philip had grown up. They had drank together on and off since their late teens. They even shared a few nights in Detox upon occasion.

"I've known you for what, fifteen years?" asked Joe, looking right into Highmountain's face, squinting as his eyes tried to focus.

Philip didn't respond right away, so Joe continued.

"Shit, Philip. You've been in jail more times than anyone I know. Hell, when you walk in the guards must ask if you want the usual, kind of like a customer or something."

Joe and Johnny laughed loudly. Highmountain smiled thinly at the joke at his expense while looking around the room. There was only one window in front looking out onto the street, but it was covered with a black film. The only light in the place came from behind the bar, the neon lights on the wall, and the small candles on the tables. It was like a dark night with no moon and only a few stars in the sky.

Philip liked the dark. It reminded him of nights at hunting camp with his uncles, sitting around campfires and telling stories. He hadn't been hunting with them in almost a decade, but he remembered the long conversations, sometimes in Indian, and the fire's radiant warmth.

The bartender came over with another round of beers. She sat them in front of each man and took some crumpled bills from the pile in the center of the table.

Philip rolled his neck, trying to loosen his tense muscles. His black hair was long and straight, and it was tied in a pony tail hanging about a foot below his shoulders.

"So what are you guys doing?" he asked.

"Hell, man," replied Joe. "You're looking at it."

The man named Johnny didn't say a word. He just nodded his head in agreement. Then he rubbed his left hand up and down his right arm like he was cold or something. He was the nervous sort. Philip had known his kind in jail, men who were always nervous, always watching their back. He didn't trust them.

"Say, Phil. You got any money?" Joe asked.

Highmountain looked down at the small pile of cash on the table.

"I got about two hundred bucks," he said. "I worked in prison sometimes and they put a little money into an account for me so that I could buy things once in a while after I paid off my restitution. It's all I've got,"

He took another drink.

"Hey," Johnny said, smiling slyly. "I bet you haven't had a woman in a while, huh?"

Joe smiled, too.

"I guess not," replied Philip.

"Hey," Johnny said to Joe who sat across from him. "Let's take him to that strip joint on Second Avenue."

Highmountain hesitated, but the other two talked him into it, and shortly after the three men were walking several blocks through early winter. When they entered the strip bar, they sat down at a table near a wooden dance floor. There were mirrors on the walls and the music was too loud. From his table, Philip watched two naked women dancing below a ballroom globe. For a few minutes he watched their writhing bodies. It was true that he hadn't been with a woman in a while, and the dancing girls reminded him it had been too long.

The Indian never liked places like these. Although

he had been in them before, always with friends, he still held them in contempt. From the bar and other tables, pathetic men drank over-priced booze while they stared at dancers or paid for lap dances. The room was smoke-filled and the women were never very good looking. Highmountain always thought such places were for fools and little-dicked men who couldn't find women of their own. They came here believing that these women really wanted them, thinking themselves so attractive that the dancers would go home with them or, better yet, the women might take them home to their sleazy, dim lit apartments for a night of free sex and companionship where something more lasting might be born from the ashes of prostitution.

When twenty dollars was laid down, a woman would dance bare-breasted, rubbing her hot, smooth flesh against the paying man who would sit still with his legs parted. Sometimes the girl raked her sweaty breasts across his cheeks, looking into his eyes as if he was somehow special, as if *he* was the one she had waited for all night long. And it would work. The men would stay all night until they were good and drunk and broke.

But after the last twenty dollar bill was spent and the last lap dance danced, the women turned their attentions elsewhere, to paying customers, and the broke men would walk out onto the windy streets alone with only a wet spot on the front of their jeans to remind them that they had ever been inside.

Two hookers were standing at the far end of the bar talking to a middle-aged, well-dressed man. Philip noticed them at the same time Johnny Kasnoff did.

"That reminds me," Johnny said, grinning.

Highmountain and Joe stopped drinking and listened.

"The other day, I was in this bar and three girls sat at the table behind me. I could hear them real good. This first girl says, 'I name by boyfriend after soda pop.' Then the other girls said that they did too.

Philip watched the naked dancer, even though he was listening to the joke. He reached down under the table and adjusted his erection.

"So the first girl says, 'I name my boyfriend Seven-Up, cause it's seven inches long and it's always up.' The second girl says, 'I call my boyfriend Mountain Dew, cause he's always trying to mount me and do me.' The third girl says, 'I call my boyfriend Jim Beam.' One of the other girls said, 'That's not soda pop. That's hard liquor.'

Philip and Joe waited for the punch line.

Johnny had a broad grin as he told that last of the joke.

"That third girl smiled real big and said, 'That's my Jimmy!'

Everyone laughed for a long time. After a while the well-dressed man left with one of the women from the bar.

Three men were sitting at the nearest table. All of

them were wearing cowboy hats and shiny leather boots, and one of them was sitting on the chair right behind Highmountain, who could hear their conversation. It wasn't that he was trying to listen, just that one of the cowboys started to speak louder, perhaps aware that the Indian was listening.

"So this guy's driving his truck through this village," the man says loud enough so that Philip can hear him above the music and the sound of other people talking.

"He picks up this Indian woman hitchhiking on the side of the road and asks where she's going."

Johnny emptied the last drink in his bottle and stuck his finger in the hole, making sounds as he pulled it out fast.

"She says she's going to the liquor store. On the way, the guy starts feeling horny and he unzips his pants and pulls out his dick."

Philip had heard lots of these kinds of jokes before, but they still bothered him.

"The Indian woman looks at the driver and says, 'You're passionate.' The guy looks down at his hard dick and says, 'Well, thank you.' The Indian woman see's what he was talking about and points out the truck window saying, 'No. The liquor store. You're pashin' it."

The three cowboys laughed and ordered another round of beers while Philip and his friends sat quietly for a long time before Joe broke the silence.

"All right," Joe nearly stuttered. "I've got a good one

to tell you guys."

Before he started the joke, Highmountain went to the bathroom to piss.

All through the night the men drank and laughed. It was a long night. After five rum and cokes and seven table dances, Philip began to float. He felt good. He forgot about prison until Johnny Kasnoff asked what he had done.

The Indian was about to answer when Joe interupted.

"Hell, Johnny, I guess you never heard about Highmountain. He's one tough bastard Indian," he said looking at the girl sitting at the table with them.

She was white and around twenty-two years old. She had brown hair cut off just below her shoulders, and she wore black panties and a thin black bra with a gold-colored zipper in the front. It was pulled halfway down and her breasts almost fell out onto the table. She told the men her name was Kei, that it rhymed with pie. Philip had already paid her for a table dance and they had seen her on stage twice. He liked the way she looked and he was excited.

The girl just smiled and drank her five dollar soda. It was one of the many scams in dives such as this. The girls weren't allowed to drink on the job, so when men offered to buy them drinks, the bartenders poured them sodas and charged the men five bucks.

Joe leaned over nearer to Kasnoff and continued his story.

"You know that bar we was in before? About two years ago Highmountain goes in there drunker than shit. He gets in a fight with two white guys and he pulls out a knife and sticks it into one of them guys. Almost killed him."

Philip didn't say anything, but closed his eyes and listened to the music. The air in the room was heavy and too warm. Philip was drunk now and he felt sick.

"You know that mirror in the bar?" Joe asked Kasnoff.

The part Indian man nodded.

"Well, Philip here threw the other man into it after he stuck the first guy. He broke the mirror, man!" he exclaimed, his voice loud with excitement.

"That's some shit," said Johnny, turning his head side to side in disbelief.

Joe was laughing now.

"Yea," he said, almost yelling above the music. "And the funny thing is, he just got out of jail a week before for robbing a liquor store!"

The two men and the girl burst out laughing, but Philip was quiet.

After a while, Highmountain stood up and walked outside. He couldn't walk straight, but he managed to find the side of the building before he threw up in the alley. He stood with his forehead against the cold wall for several minutes, breathing in the icy night air to clear his head. It didn't help much.

Philip reached into his pocket and pulled out his money. There was one twenty dollar bill. He searched his other pockets. They were empty.

It was late and he was tired. Without saying goodbye to his friends he walked uptown, passing other drunks on the neon-lit streets, to the Catholic homeless shelter where he was offered a cot and a blanket. It was warm inside and filled with the sound of many men sleeping and snoring and farting. The Indian slept badly all night, tossing on the small cot and falling off it twice. When he finally fell asleep for good, he dreamed of home in his village.

At first he saw himself fishing with his dad and uncle. They worked all summer catching fish and putting away meat for the winter. They trapped for furs which his dad sold in town in the fall. In his dream, Philip heard the sound of the river and the wind, and he felt the sun warm on his face. He saw his friends, too. Then he began to dream of his cousin, Kenny, and he began to sweat.

They had never been too close, Philip and Kenny, but they saw each other often. It was a pretty small community. Sometimes Kenny and his dad came down to help Philip and his father cut fish. But still, Philip thought, Kenny was alright. Most of the time he was quiet. Kenny's dad was always drunk. Philip couldn't remember a time when he wasn't. Philip knew some Indians are funny when they get drunk and some get plain mean.

Whenever Kenny's dad was drunk he became mean. Real mean.

One time when his dad was drunk, Kenny's mom tried to pull the keys out of their old Dodge Econoline's ignition so that he couldn't drive. They yelled at each other for a while, and then his dad rolled up the van's window and his mom's arm got stuck. Kenny and Philip watched as his dad turned the radio's volume up as high as it went, shifted into drive, and took off down the road, dragging his mother in a cloud of dust and flinging rocks. Kenny and Philip stood and listened to her screaming and crying until the van vanished around a bend.

Kenny walked home one Saturday afternoon in July years later when he was twenty-three, went inside his small house, brought out a lever-action rifle he used to hunt big game, jacked a round into the chamber, and sat down on the porch alone under a hot summer sun.

Philip found him later that day. The back of Kenny's head was all over the dark red wall behind him.

Highmountain awoke suddenly and sat up on the small metal cot which creaked when he moved. He was sweating and he could barely breathe. After his eyes focused, he saw where he was. The Indian sat for a long time listening to the sounds of other men sleeping. After a while, Philip looked at his watch and then he stood up, put on his clothes, and walked out into the night where the city was sleeping restfully.

"In the beginning time, way long ago, when Raven created the world, he made rivers so that they flowed both ways. You could go upriver on one side and go downriver on the other side. Later, though, Raven decided that it was too easy for people, so he made them flow only downriver."

Chapter 2

It was early morning when the sun rose above the mountains, its orange light reflecting from the windows of tall buildings downtown. Philip had been walking the streets for hours before he stopped at a soup kitchen to eat a free breakfast. He had been there before when he was broke, which was most of the time.

He sat alone at a small table near a window where he could look out onto the street where cars began to line the avenues. The city was coming alive, and people began to move in and out of shops and offices. It was cold outside and the people were bundled up in heavy coats, and they held their hands over their ears as they ran from their vehicles into the many buildings.

The place was nearly full, but the Indian sat alone. When an old black man tried to sit at the table, Philip put his foot on the empty chair.

"Can't sit here," he said to the man.

The old man with gray hair stared at the Indian, then turned and looked around. He saw a vacant table on the far side of the room and shuffled over to it with his tray of pancakes and scrambled eggs. When he sat down, he turned to look back at the Indian before drowning his eggs in ketchup.

Highmountain was finishing his second cup of coffee when he saw someone familiar walk through the door and stand in the meal line. The man was also Indian, and Philip poured more cream into his cup while he watched him load his tray with food. He was older than Highmountain, and he had a sparse black mustache.

At the front of the line the man took an orange from a large basket and then walked into the dining area where he saw Highmountain sitting by the window alone.

"Philip!" he yelled, as he walked over to the table and sat his tray on the red and white checkered vinyl tablecloth.

"Where you been, Phil?" he asked, sitting down at the table.

"You got any money, Nick?" Highmountain asked, setting down his empty cup.

"Hell, Phil. I wouldn't be eating here if I had cash," the other Indian said, while pouring syrup over his pancakes.

Philip took the orange from the other man's tray and began to peel it while he spoke.

"Say, Nick. You seen Sue lately?"

"I saw her maybe this spring," he said. "She heard you was in jail again for fighting or something."

Philip looked out the window.

"Did she ask about me?" he asked after a while without looking at his friend.

Nick shoved a sausage in his mouth just before he began to speak.

"No. Not really," he said while wiping his mouth with his shirt sleeve. "But she had Mikey with her. He looked good."

Philip hadn't seen Mikey in almost three years and he tried to imagine what he looked like.

"How old is he now?" Nick asked. "Must be around six."

Highmountain finished peeling the orange and pulled off a wedge.

"He's five last month," he said, sliding the wedge into his mouth.

The other man ate his breakfast while Philip stared out the window at the mountains in the distance.

Philip had known Sue since they were young. When she was only four years old, her parents died in a accident when their jon boat struck a submerged log and sank into the swift, silty waters of the river. After that, she lived in the village with her grandmother who taught her their language. They lived in a small log cabin downriver a mile or two from where Philip lived. She had always been pretty, but Philip never paid much attention to her back then because he was several years older than she was.

Six years earlier he spent a summer in the village working for relatives. He hadn't seen Sue in a long time. Maybe eight or nine years. She was home from college for the summer. Sue had always been real smart and everyone knew that she'd be a good teacher. After graduating, her plans were to return to her village and teach in the small school.

One evening a potlatch was held in honor of an elder who had died the week before. A potlatch is a day long ceremony of communal meals and dancing. Highmountain had been to many in his life. Late in the night, members of the deceased's clan gives away gifts of blankets, rifles, and cash to non-clan members present at the potlatch. At some later potlatch, those who received gifts would be the ones giving them away. It was an old tradition of reciprocity designed to strengthen the bond between clans.

When Philip first saw Sue at the potlatch dance, he couldn't believe his eyes. Sue had always been kind of skinny and short when they were kids. She wasn't that way now, and he had to ask someone who the woman was who had walked through the community hall's doors.

"Who's that?" Highmountain asked the teenage boy sitting beside him while pointing at the beautiful woman who was standing just inside the doorway, looking around the large room. After a minute, she walked across the planked floors to the other side of the great hall.

The boy had to speak loudly to be heard above the sound of drums and the elders singing.

"Oh, That's Sue Pete," he said.

Philip watched her for a long time. Sue was magnificent. She was perhaps twenty-three years old, Philip thought, and she looked to him to be just under six feet tall. She had high cheek bones, and her long black hair was pulled back by a beaded black leather hair pin. Sue was no longer the skinny young girl he had known in his youth. She was formidable in a way, but not threatening. She was powerful, but she moved with the easy gate of a wolf. She had strong bones and large breasts, and she wore a dark brown leather vest over her blue shirt and dark blue jeans.

Sue was what they called in the village, "kasuun." Beautiful.

Philip watched her all night. He watched as she sat along the walls of the hall talking to elders and watching the dancers. Sometimes she danced with the other women in the outside ring around where older and younger men danced in the center, stomping so forcefully that the very foundation shook. He watched everything she did and he loved the way her body and hands moved when she danced.

A week later one of Highmountain's cousins invited him to a party along the river. A dozen Indians were already there, standing around a large fire on a sand bar. Beyond the flames and rising sparks, the river ran to the sea, carving new channels and slowly polishing boulders. It was a highway for salmon to the many tributaries and lakes north of the village where the fish, tired and spent, emptied their determined lives onto sand and gravel.

All around were cases of beer and everyone had a can in hand. Some of the people were too young to drink, but nobody cared. Philip knew from experience that everyone drank. Everyone drank and everyone died, and salmon filled the river in summer. That was the way of things.

Around midnight a car pulled up and parked beside the other cars and trucks in the field. Three young women got out and began to walk the fifty or so yards to the gathering.

From where he stood, Philip could see that one of them was Sue.

His heart raced. He was nervous. In all his life he had never known a more powerful and beautiful woman. He wanted her more than anything, especially since his cousin had told him that she was single. And it wasn't all sexual. There was something about her that moved his heart, and Philip wanted to be part of who she was.

When the three young women were close, someone handed them beers and they joined in the conversations around the fire. Everyone talked for hours, telling jokes and gossiping about other people. Throughout the long night, many people left, but new people always replaced them. By the time the fire finally consumed its pile of driftwood, all of the cases of beer were gone. The party had been a blast and everyone was drunk. A boy named Jimmy, drunk and in a stupor, was sleeping on the sand beside the current. A slight breeze kept the mosquitos down.

Once Sue had seen Philip, she came over to where he stood. They talked for hours about the old days, and she told him how she and her friend Britta had just hitchhiked to Mexico and back. She had lost her wallet about two days before they crossed the border, and she couldn't prove that she was American. Being Indian didn't help much. Her brown skin, black hair and dark eyes made her look Mexican. The broad *sombrero* she was wearing didn't help either. Britta had bought it for her in Tijuana as a souvenir.

The Border Patrol held her for a long time until she made a scene, screaming in English and at times in Indian that she wasn't Mexican. Eventually, they had to call her home to have a copy of identification faxed before they let her cross onto American soil, where she was born and where her ancestors had lived and died for thousands of years in the shadows of mountains.

When the party finally broke up, Philip gave Sue a ride because her friends had left hours earlier. Both he and Sue were drunk, and Philip could hardly keep the truck on the rough, narrow country road.

Sue sat beside him on the truck seat, even though there was plenty of room on the bench. She sat close to him and when the truck hit a bump she held onto his arm tight. Philip liked the way it felt. When they came out on the main road which led back to town and to Sue's house, Philip turned the other direction and Sue didn't say anything. After less than a mile he turned onto a road which led to a gravel pit and stopped the engine.

Highmountain's heart was pounding and his hands trembled when he turned and kissed her on the mouth. Sue had full lips. They were full and red and he wanted to press his mouth against them more than anything. They kissed for a long time and she held his long hair bunched in a tight fist. Philip unfastened her top shirt button and slid his left hand beneath the fabric. Her breast felt smooth in his strong brown hand, and he brushed his fingertips across her nipple, which hardened to his touch.

Highmountain wanted to see all of Sue, and the younger woman watched as his shaking hands unfastened all of her buttons and gently pulled back her thin blouse to expose her breasts. When Philip was finished, he looked up into the woman's dark eyes staring softly into his own. Sue pulled off Philip's shirt and then he lay upon her on the vinyl bench seat, their smooth, naked bellies warm against the other's. Highmountain loved the way his flesh felt on hers.

Philip had never wanted a woman more than he wanted Sue, and they made love on the truck seat with the radio playing quietly, while a breeze outside blew through the open windows. It was over quickly because of the beer, and Highmountain was mad at himself. His lovemaking always ended like that, and although he wanted to do it again, he was too tired and drunk to try, so he drove her home while she buttoned her shirt.

They didn't speak on the ride to her grandmother's small log cabin until he dropped her off and she told him goodnight. She gave him one brief kiss before she vanished behind the heavy wooden door.

They didn't see each other again that summer. Philip was arrested six days later for breaking into a house and stealing some guns. He went to jail for three months. When he got out he didn't go back to the village because everyone knew what he had done.

Since that summer, Philip had been incarcerated several other times. Each time his life travelled further away from the small village at the river's edge. Each conviction took him further away from Sue.

But he wanted to see her again.

There was a pay telephone near the entrance to the soup kitchen. Highmountain placed his coffee cup beside his plate on the plastic tray and carried it over to the counter where the dishwasher was busy cleaning the morning's mess. Then he went over to the phone and looked through the thick city directory. There were eight Pete's listed in the book, but only one Sue Pete. Philip ripped the thin white page from its binding and walked out onto the noisy street where he looked at the paper again, folded it, and stuffed it into his back pocket.

The Indian looked east away from the downtown center and the heavy traffic, and he began to walk along the busy sidewalk, determined to see Sue and his son again.

"Having tricked the great Chief by turning himself into the man's grandson, Raven stole the stars, the moon, and the sun from three carved boxes and released them through the smokehole. It was too late when the Chief realized what had happened."

Chapter 3

It was late morning and a young Indian boy, about five years old, was playing outside an apartment building when a strange man turned from the sidewalk and walked towards him. The boy didn't recognize the man, but he wasn't afraid of him either. Most likely the man was visiting someone in the building. After all, the skinny boy thought, lots of people lived here, so he went back to playing with his sled.

A tall shadow fell across the snow and the child's sled. The boy looked up. The stranger was standing over him, looking down and smiling. The man was also Indian, and he had long black hair tied back into a ponytail. The boy smiled back. His face was messy as though he had just eaten spaghetti, and he was missing his two front teeth. The boy's hair was black too, only shorter than the tall man's standing before him.

They were alone in the front of the building.

"Hello," the boy said, still smiling. "Did you see me sledding?"

The man said nothing, but took his hands out of his pants pockets and reached inside his dark leather jacket. He pulled out something square and thin and bent over to hand it to the child whose eyebrows knit together for an instant, trying to think what it might be. The boy smiled again after he saw what it was the man had handed him.

"Wow! Basketball cards!" he said happily as he received the gift.

There were three packs and the man, smiling silently, watched as the boy opened all of them after he had pulled off his mittens and tossed them onto the snow beside his red plastic sled.

"Are all these for me?" the boy asked.

Although his mother bought him toys when she could, they were few and far in between. The sled was the first toy he had been given in several months. Christmas was still more than a month away. Some of the other boys at preschool brought sports trading cards to school with them, but he never had any of his own. Now he could show them and maybe they'd let him play with them.

"Yep," the tall Indian said. "They're for you."

The boy picked up his mittens and looked up at the visitor.

"What's your name?" he asked.

The tall Indian rubbed his hands together and hesitated before he spoke.

"Philip," he answered.

There was something familiar about the man's voice. Maybe it wasn't his voice, the boy thought. Maybe it was his face. He wasn't certain which it was. Perhaps both. His mother had always told him not to talk to strangers, but this man didn't seem strange.

The boy introduced himself as Mikey, and then he slid the cards into his snowsuit pants. After replacing his mittens, he picked up his sled's yellow rope and walked up a small rise in the apartment's yard from where he could sled downhill for a short distance.

"You want to come?" the boy yelled back to the man who was still standing where they had first met, looking at the windows of the old brown and white building which was three stories tall and needed new paint.

Philip had seen himself in the boy's brown face from the moment they first began to speak. He knew this was his son.

"Sure," Philip said as he walked over to the small hill. "Sure, Mikey. I'll sled with you a while."

Sue Pete was in the laundry room washing clothes. She had told her son to go outside and play after she helped him put on his winter clothes and boots. There was only one laundry room on this floor and sometimes she had to wait for days until she could use the washers and dryers.

The machines were almost always loaded with other tenant's clothing.

She closed the lid to the rusted washing machine and pushed the quarter holder hard because she knew it stuck sometimes. As water began to fill the tub, she ran her hand across her forehead wiping away sweat. The room was always hot from the dryers and it smelled from bleach and detergent. Sue picked up her two empty baskets and walked down the hall to her small apartment.

Sue had moved to the city two years ago after her grandmother died. There were few jobs in the village, and she had no other relatives to live with. She came to the city to find work so she could raise Mikey. But her life wasn't going as planned. Rent was high and she could barely afford food and the heating bill. It didn't help matters that Mikey was born sick and needed lots of medical attention when he was an infant.

His sickness was her fault and Sue knew it. Sometimes she cried at night until her pillow was soaked and she had to get another one, but she never let her son see her when she was like that. She tried to make his life happy.

After Sue became pregnant, she began to drink heavily. She never did drink much before, she remembered. Sometimes she drank at parties. But she rarely got drunk, at least not until that summer night she got pregnant in the front seat of a pick-up truck. She didn't find out until months later after she returned to school.

The food in the cafeteria was plentiful and she always ate three big meals every day. She thought the weight she put on in the first months was from eating too much, and she dismissed her missed periods as a consequence of stress.

Her college courses were tough, but she liked the challenge. Halfway through the fall semester, though, Sue knew that she was pregnant. Her friends at school told her to get an abortion. But that wasn't the way of her people. Besides, many of her village girlfriends had babies while they were young. Sometimes while they were still in high school. Sue tried to keep up with her classes, but by the end of the semester she was too far behind and ended up incompleting most of them. She went back to the village during Christmas Break. She never went back to the university. Sue stayed with her grandmother and together they watched as her belly grew taut while her esteem and future appeared to vanish. At least that's how she felt.

During those last several months Sue escaped her depression by drinking, which only made things worse. She began indiscreetly with beers at village parties where she wore thick parkas and sweaters to hide her condition. After a while, though, she drank the hard stuff alone in her small room. She slept in later and later each week, but her grandmother thought it was because of the baby. After she awoke in late mornings, Sue smuggled empty bottles out of the small house so that her grandmother wouldn't see them, and she kept her window open on cold mornings to blow out the smell of stale beer cans and empty bottles of whiskey and vodka. Sue used what was left of her college loan to fuel her drinking binges, and fortunately or not, the money ran out about the time she had her baby.

When Mikey was born, he wanted the same kind of bottle his mother had wanted. He was born too soon and his tiny body shook so hard that Sue couldn't stand to hold him. He had other problems too, the kind found in the lives of all alcoholic infants. He screamed and screamed all through the night. The doctors helped him what little they could, but it was hard for both Sue and her baby in his first year in the village along the river.

The apartment was small and had only one bedroom. There was a single bed against one wall and another along the opposite wall. There were a few pictures on the white-painted wall, mostly of her grandmother and Mikey. A thin line ran vertically up the wall from where the sheetrock had cracked, and the carpet was stained from previous owners and from where her son had spilled drinks or food on the floor. The apartment was always too cold in the winter. Sue could only wash laundry once in a while, but it was the only place she could afford. Besides, it was close to the restaurant down the street where she worked as a waitress six days a week.

Sue sat down the empty laundry basket on the small kitchen table and looked at her watch. She had twenty minutes until the wash would be done. She checked the fish soup on the stove and looked out the window to see where her son was. Mikey was playing on a snow berm which the city's snow plows had pushed there from the street and sidewalks. Sue watched for a minute as he trudged up the pile towing his sled and then sled down the other side. He was bundled up in winter clothes and she could see that he was happy.

Someone was standing nearby talking to her son. From the third floor window Sue couldn't see who it was. Whoever it was was standing with their back to the building and had a long black ponytail. Sue watched as the person sat down in the back of the sled and went down the small hill with her son in the front. At the bottom they both rolled off the red sled as though they had crashed. Sue could see Mikey was laughing when he stood up and brushed snow from his pants.

When the person with her young son stood up and turned around towards the snow pile, Sue could see that it was an Indian man. She wasn't sure who it was. He was too far away for her to make out his features. She thought that she recognized him, though, and she looked closer until her eyes widened. It was Philip. Sue ran across the room and into the hall. In her hurry, she didn't close the apartment door. She ran down the flights of stairs fast, not stopping until she was at the main door where she stopped and looked hard again at the man with her son as she tried to catch her breath. It was Philip Highmountain. She hadn't seen him in three years, but it was him. He was playing with Mikey alone.

Sue ran out across the snow wearing only socks on her feet. She grabbed her son and told him to go inside the house.

"I don't want to go in yet!" Mikey protested, trying to break free of his mother's grip. "I'm not cold, Mom."

But Sue held his hand tight and led him towards the door.

"Mom!" he yelled. "My sled," he said turning and pointing to his plastic sled lying in the snow beside the man.

"I'll get it for you later," Sue told her son when they were on the sidewalk near the front door.

Mikey was still trying to break loose of his mother's grip.

"But I was playing with my new friend," he said.

Sue pushed opened the heavy wood and glass door and told Mikey to go upstairs to their apartment and to get ready for a bath. After she watched her son walk up a flight of stairs, Sue turned and walked back outside. She stopped several yards from the taller man and grabbed the sled's yellow rope. Then she stood up and faced the man. Her socks were soaked through and her feet were cold, but her face was red.

"What the hell are you doing here?" she screamed at the Indian.

Philip put his hands into his pockets and shrugged his shoulders before he spoke.

"I just wanted to see Mikey," he said calmly, trying to diffuse the situation.

Sue took a step closer to him.

"You want to see him after three years? And you only saw him once before that!" she yelled.

"Come on, Sue. He's my son, too," Highmountain said.

It was obvious to Philip that Sue was about to blow up. Her face wasn't beautiful like it was at the potlatch or when they met that night at the party along the river's edge. It was red and angry and poisonous. Philip readied himself for what came next.

"Your son? Shit, Philip. You've been in jail almost his entire life. What kind of father are you? You've never spent a dollar to help me raise him. He's not your son! "

Highmountain took a small step back while looking at the ground between them where his and Mikey's footprints led towards the snow hill. He noticed that Sue wasn't wearing shoes.

"You never did nothing for him. He doesn't even know you," Sue said. Then her face took on another expression. It wasn't anger. It was more like horror.

"You didn't tell him you're his father, did you?" she asked. Her voice was lower than before, just above a whisper.

"I didn't say nothing like that, Sue," Philip said slowly. "I just wanted to see Mikey again. You know I haven't seen him in years."

Sue remembered the last time he saw Mikey. It wasn't good. Philip came by late one night drunk and smelling of beer. When Sue saw him outside the cabin she didn't know what to do. Highmountain knocked on the door, and she didn't answer it until he knocked for so long that she knew he wasn't going away. Mikey was asleep at first, but the noise woke him and he started crying. When he heard the child crying, Philip knew that Sue was home and he knocked even louder while yelling from outside the locked door.

When she finally let him in, Philip started talking about the future. He told her that they should get married and raise their son together. But Sue knew he had no job and no prospects of one. Besides, she knew he had just gotten out of jail for the third or fourth time. Maybe the fifth. She couldn't remember how many times or why, and she didn't care to know anyhow. When Mikey walked into the small kitchen, Philip picked him up and threw him into the air over and over, catching him under his arms each time he came down. Sue begged him to put her son down, but Philip didn't listen. He kept throwing the little boy up and up until Mikey threw up on him and began to scream.

Sue wrestled her son from Highmountain and yelled at him to leave. They argued for a long time above the sound of their son's crying, but Philip knew he was losing and finally left. Sue slammed the door hard and locked it.

She held Mikey close for a long time singing his favorite songs until he fell asleep again.

Sue's voice became loud again after remembering his last visit.

"You stay away from us. Stay away from me. I don't want you. Do you hear me?" she demanded, her voice so loud that an old woman walking on the sidewalk stopped to see what was the commotion.

"Mikey doesn't need you either," she continued. "You already ruined my life. He's got enough problems. He doesn't need you to fuck up his life any more than it already is."

Philip looked at Sue's mouth as she spoke. He probably deserved every word she said, but he had never heard them spoken to him before. In his own mind he must have thought that things weren't really all that bad. After all, most of his friends in the village drank too much, and many of them went to jail for one thing or another. Maybe not as often as he did, but he didn't think he was all that bad.

"I really just wanted to see him. See how big he is. What he looked like. That's all," Philip said, his voice much calmer than Sue's.

"You've seen him. Ok? Now go away. Just go. We don't want you. *He* doesn't want you."

These last words hurt Highmountain. They cut into his heart like a knife and made him feel very sad. He knew that Sue wouldn't want him to see Mikey, but he wasn't prepared for this. He thought maybe they could work things out. Make things better.

He was wrong.

Sue turned and began to walk towards the apartment building's front door, dragging the long red sled behind her. She stopped after only a few steps and turned to speak to Philip one last time.

"If you bother us again, I swear I'll take Mikey and move away so that you never find us. You hear me? Just leave us alone!"

Highmountain stood in the snow-covered yard for a long time, looking at the rows of windows facing him and at the small hill covered with the many tracks he and his son had left in the new snow together. He saw how they intertwined, how their tracks crossed only here and there. After a while he walked to the sidewalk and headed towards the downtown skyline two miles distant. It was cold and the Indian felt the lonely chill of winter on his face and ears as he walked on alone, only his lean and empty shadow before him as company.

"After Raven tricked Whale into opening his mouth, the little black bird ran straight down the giant throat with a packsack of wood. Inside, Raven cut pieces of meat from the whale and roasted it over a small fire. He stayed there a long time until he had eaten everything."

Chapter 4

It was almost noon when Highmountain reached downtown again. The sun, which was up for only a few hours each day now, was already past its peak, slowly sinking in the sky below a rising moon. The city streets were congested with automobiles and pedestrians going home for lunch or to one of the many small cafes and restaurants which lined the bustling streets.

Philip was still thinking of Sue and Mikey when he turned onto an alley. It was a shortcut which he had used often. Along the narrow row were the back doors to bars and stores where merchandise and supplies were unloaded from trucks. In the summer, the doors would be open, but now, in early winter, they were closed tight. There were no windows along the alley.

Highmountain saw a coin beside a dark green dumpster outside the back door of a pull tab place. He walked closer and saw that it was a half dollar.

"Someone must have dropped it last night or this morning in the dark," he thought, as he bent over to collect the money, feeling that his luck was changing.

When he stood up, he saw three men at the far end of the alley. Two of the men wore cowboy hats, and all three wore cowboy boots and heavy, dark coats. Highmountain recognized them from the bar the night before. They were coming his way and talking to each other. They were too far away and Philip couldn't hear what they were saying, but the one without a hat kept looking behind him as if he was expecting something, or someone.

As they began to pass, all four men nodded a kind of affirmation of one another's existence. Then the cowboys stopped and one of them grabbed Philip's arm.

"Got any cigarettes, Indian?" the man asked. The other two men looked nervously up and down the cold, vacant alley. They were alone except for a brood of ravens around the garbage bin where the coin had been.

The Indian shook his head.

"No, man. I ain't got no cigarettes on me. Sorry," he said as he pulled his arm free and turned to continue down the alley.

The men circled close around Highmountain.

The tallest of the three, the one without a hat, spoke again.

"You got any cash on you?" he asked, stepping so close that Philip could smell the Red Man he was chewing.

"I ain't got nothing," he replied, as he turned his head slightly and tried to back away from the man and his bad breath.

Just then the other two men, both behind him, grabbed his arms and pulled back on them until they hurt. The man without a hat pulled out a knife and held it close to Philip's face.

"I wanna see what you got, Indian," he said while one of the men behind him removed Highmountain's wallet from his pants backpocket and looked inside, throwing the folded white phone book page with Sue's address onto the ground, where the wind blew it behind the green dumpster.

"Shit," the man said. "There's only ten damn bucks in here."

The cowboy with the knife brought the blade closer to Highmountain's face until it touched his chin.

"You better have more than that," he whispered as he leaned towards the Indian.

"Let's see what's inside your coat pocket," the cowboy said as he reached with his other hand to open Philip's leather jacket.

Highmountain had been in plenty of fights in his life. He won most of them, but the ones he lost were bad. He had been hospitalized a few times, and he had sent people to the hospital. One of the times Philip was in prison, an older, bigger prisoner became more than slightly interested in him. Philip knew what the older man wanted, having seen how some men preyed on weak new-comers and loners.

One day, Highmountain was working in the laundry service when the man came in with a friend. They tried to hold him down, but Philip smashed the big man's head against an industrial washing machine and crushed his skull. The other man wasn't as big as his friend, and he was stunned at Philip's strength. He wasn't prepared to fight the Indian alone, and Philip broke two of the man's ribs and an arm.

Highmountain lost three months of good behavior time for the incident, but it was worth it. No one bothered him again. In fact, most of the inmates called him "Chief" from then on. He didn't really like it, but it was better than a boot to the head or being sodomized.

When the hatless cowboy reached into Philip's leather jacket to feel the inside pockets, the Indian raised his knee as fast and hard as he could into the man's groin. The cowboy dropped his knife and fell to his knees. Before the other two men knew what to do, Highmountain stomped on the foot of the man who had his wallet, smashing his toes.

The man dropped the wallet and let go of the Indian, who quickly punched the other man in the side of his face. But before Philip could get away, the man with the smashed toe grabbed his long hair and held him. In a second, the other man began punching Highmountain in the stomach and chest while the hatless cowboy tried to stand up, still clutching his groin.

At that moment a freight truck turned into the alley. The driver must have seen the fight. He pushed hard on the truck's horn as he bore the large diesel down on all four men.

One of the cowboys grabbed Philip's wallet from the ground, and then all three turned and ran down the alley, leaving the Indian alone holding his side with one hand.

Highmountain looked around him for his wallet. It was gone, but the man's knife was laying in the snow. He picked it up and limped towards the truck.

"You all right?" the truck driver asked, leaning out his window.

Highmountain looked up at the man for only a second.

"I'm okay," he said, as he walked past the truck and out of the alley onto a busy sidewalk.

The Indian walked the streets for a while. His belly and ribs ached from the punches and he felt a chill creeping through him. Philip went in and out of several stores to get warm. But mostly he used the time to think. He was already tired of the city. Tired of everything about it. Village life was simpler. Safer. Highmountain wanted to go home, but he had no money. He had spent ten dollars to buy the gifts for Mikey, and the city cowboys stole the rest. He didn't understand men like that. Especially not here.

"The closest a man like that comes to being a cowboy," Philip thought, "is when he takes a whiz in the bathroom at an Arby's."

The Indian smiled at his own joke.

Highmountain was sure that he wanted to go home. He was tired and alone, and he knew that Sue would never let him see his son again. He had no money and no way to get home. But he would go home, of that much he was certain.

He would find a way.

"After Raven pulled out Cormorant's tongue, he went back to the village and told the people that it was he, not Cormorant, who caught all the fish in the canoe. When the other bird started jumping up and down waving his wings, Raven told the villagers that he was trying to tell them how great a fisher Raven was."

Chapter 5

A tall Indian walked into the store. He had been standing outside looking in through the window for almost fifteen minutes, holding his jacket collar high against his flush cheeks for warmth. When he came through the glass and chrome-trimmed door, an electronic chime announced his arrival, like the call of geese flying low overhead on their way south for the winter. He wore a worn black leather jacket, faded blue jeans with a tear across one knee, and he had long hair. He looked like he was at least thirty years old, maybe older.

Tom Hancock saw a lot of Natives in his shop. Sometimes they came from far villages to sell furs trapped during winter which he had made into expensive coats, hats, and parkas. Others came in to sell carved ivory and antlers or beadwork. Sometimes they came in just to browse. Most often, though, they came through the door, tired and drunk, setting off the chime simply to escape the city's cold.

Hancock watched the tall Indian in the curved mirror just above the entrance, watched him looking at the many parkas and coats trimmed with wolf and wolverine fur displayed in the window. There were only a few people inside. It was near closing and the customers would leave soon. It had been a slow day. Business was always slow after the summer tourists returned home.

The store was one large room with several rows of gifts and art and fur coats and Eskimo parkas separated by wide aisles. The place smelled of tanned leather, and there were animal heads and stuffed fish mounted high on the pine-clad walls.

The salesman watched the man from a distance. Natives rarely bought anything here. Besides, nowadays, only tourists could afford most of the gifts and souvenirs anyhow. The art and furs were bought from Natives, but they were sold to tourists and rich oil industry executives.

Thinking the Indian to be only a vagrant seeking relief from the cold and wind outside, Hancock approached him.

"May I help you?" he asked.

Tom was short and balding. He wore a black vest over his dark blue shirt and slacks which looked of seventies vintage.

The Indian didn't answer. Instead, he nervously looked around the room. Just then the chime announced the departure of a customer. Hancock and the Indian were alone now.

"Are you waiting for a bus or something?" Tom asked, annoyed that the man didn't respond to his first question.

It wasn't that Hancock didn't like Indians. Tom had grown up near a reservation, and many of his childhood friends were Indians. He remembered summer vacations when he was a teenager. Billy Darkhorse was his best friend back then. His parents ran the only gas station on the reservation, so Billy grew up knowing cars. He fixed up an old pick up truck in his dad's garage after school. It was a year long project, but the truck was pretty fast when it was finished. He couldn't get the manifold to fit right, so the engine was really loud.

Billy had a younger brother named Sherman, who was almost as big as Billy. Sherman was a halfbreed and the other kids always teased him about his white father. Sometimes they picked up some friends from school and cruised the backroads. One of their friends had an older brother who was old enough to buy beer. The boys all pitched in enough to get a case of beer, and they would drive around until the beer was gone and it was time to go home. Billy always kept a baseball bat behind his seat. It was light colored and there were chips in the wood.

He said it was for protection, but they never saw him get into a fight. Mostly they used it to smash mailboxes as they sped down the highway, each boy taking turns swinging as they passed driveways at fifty or sixty miles an hour. Over two summers, Tom remembered, they must have destroyed three hundred mailboxes. People who lived along the highway and backcountry roads started building their mailboxes stronger and farther from the road, which annoyed the postman who had to reach way out of his window whenever he delivered mail.

Billy always drove the black truck while the others stayed in the truckbed, trying not to fall out when it hit bumps on the road or turned sharp corners. The truck only had an AM radio, and the local stations played either religious music or country. It wasn't much of a choice, but it was better than nothing. So they listened to loud country music through the even louder sound of the engine.

Once, Tom recalled, he had to piss really bad after drinking four beers. He could still see it in his mind. It was one of those clear memories in which he would never forget the smell of the air or the color of the sky and clouds. It was one of those memories he carried forever to remind him in old age that he was once young and foolish and beautiful.

"Billy!" he yelled at the driver's window which was rolled halfway down. "I need to take a leak!"

The truck didn't slow down and Billy never let on that he had heard him.

Tom leaned closer to the window and pounded on the roof.

"I got to piss, man!" he yelled. "Come on, pull over!"

Sherman yelled to Tom from the opposite side of the truck bed, the wind racing through his long black hair.

"Do it over the side, Tommy!" he yelled. "Do it over the side," he said again, gesturing with his right hand what he meant.

Tom went to the back of the truck near the tailgate where he unzipped his pants and tried to go. The truck was going fast and the road was bumpy. He tried to steady himself with his left hand on the side rail, but it was hard to keep his footing. For a moment the road was smoother and he began to piss. He remembered how good it felt, and he watched the water spraying on the hot pavement, leaving a long streak down the highway. Another car was gaining on them and Tommy tried to urinate faster. He had drunk four beers in the truck with his friends, and he had had a soda before they left. The ride was so bumpy that he would start a stream and after only a few seconds he would have to stop the flow, trying to steady himself so he wouldn't fall.

The other boys in the truck bed were laughing.

"You having problems Hand-cock?" one boy yelled out above the loud exhaust, stressing the two syllables of Tom's last name.

Then Sherman jumped into the teasing.

"What's the matter, Tommy? Don't you know how to piss yet?"

Everyone was laughing, even Billy, who could see

Tommy in the rearview mirror.

Tommy tried to get it all out. When a stream finally came, Billy started turning the steering wheel left and right. The paper thin river of urine looked like a long shiny snake splattered on the highway. Then one of the boys leaned close to the driver's window and spoke to Billy, who pressed on the brakes so hard that Tommy fell backward into the truckbed. His fly was still open and piss splashed all over the place, including on himself. He tried to scramble to his feet, but each time Billy kept speeding up and slamming on the brakes until Tommy was soaked.

When he went home that night his parents didn't smell the beer on his breath.

Two summers later, Billy and Sherman worked with Tom on a forest fire crew. While cutting a firebreak a half mile ahead of a five hundred acre forest fire, another worker's chainsaw kicked back and sliced into Sherman's stomach, ripping his shirt open and cutting the skin beneath just deep enough that his intestines poured out. The accident happened so quickly that Sherman didn't realize what happened right away. When the realization came, he screamed so loudly that the other firefighters heard him even above the sound of their own chainsaws. The leafy earth around him was bright red, and blood was dripping off branches nearby when they found him lying on the ground screaming, his eyes wild, holding his guts close to him, trying to keep them off the ground. The chainsaw was still idling beside him, its sharp-toothed chain turning slowly on the shiny steel bar while the man who cut him threw up all over himself.

Billy and Tom carried him out to a truck and drove him twenty-six miles to the nearest medical center. They pushed his organs into their cavity and tried to stop the bleeding with their shirts, but Sherman lost a lot of blood and passed out halfway. They pushed their shirts hard against the wound and Billy tried to hold the skin around the jagged gash closed like an envelope. The chain had ripped his skin badly, but it didn't damage a single organ.

Later, in the hospital, Sherman said that he was surprised how warm and smooth his guts felt in his hands as he tried to stuff himself back together.

Tom hadn't seen Sherman since the fall of that year, nearly twenty years ago.

The Indian in the shop reminded Tom of his summers with Billy Darkhorse. But this man wasn't Billy and he ignored his questions and walked to the back of the store where the cash register sat on a dark wood counter.

Tom had been following close behind the man, and he cut in front of him when they reached the counter.

"Can I help you?" he asked anxiously, trying to hold his ground.

The Indian reached into his back pocket and pulled out a knife. Tom saw that the blade was only about five inches long, but it was enough to catch his attention.

"I want all your money," the man said, holding the knife at the salesman's neck. " Open the register."

For an instant Tom looked towards the front door. His wife usually came in around quiting time to help clean up and close the till. But at that moment no one came in. Outside on the street an old pick up truck like Billy's passed the front window and vanished.

The Indian, who was much taller than he was, moved a step closer and pressed his blade against the short salesman's neck just beneath his chin. Tom began to sweat and his blue shirt suddenly turned black under his arms.

For an instant he hoped that his wife wouldn't come through the door. He didn't want her to find him lying on the carpet in a pool of blood with one hand gripped around his ripped throat, trying to hold in life. Tom remembered the way he and Billy tried to stop Sherman's blood in the back of the pickup.

Hancock tried to speak, but he stuttered at first. "All, all, alright. I'll ope, open it," he said, walking around to the other side of the counter.

Tom only stuttered when he was really nervous, and he hadn't stuttered at all since he was twenty. It surprised him that he couldn't get the words out.

The Indian stayed beside him with the knife blade pushed against the salesman's back.

Tom pushed a few keys on the register and the black drawer opened. It was full of cash. Mostly tens and twenties. There were quite a few checks under the drawer and a several fifties. The Indian grabbed the pile, took out the fifty dollars bills and threw the checks onto the carpet.

"What else you got here?" the Indian asked, pointing the knife at the salesman's chest. "You got a wallet?"

Tom nodded.

"Give it to me," the Indian demanded.

There wasn't much cash in his wallet, maybe fifteen or sixteen dollars, which the Indian took and then he tossed the wallet onto the floor beside the checks.

"You, you have ever, everything," Tom tried to say. "Ok? Now you can go."

The Indian stuffed the wad of bills into his front pants pocket and took a step back. He turned to leave and took a few steps. Hancock was relieved that it was over and that he hadn't been hurt. He was thankful that his wife hadn't come in yet.

Then the Indian stopped and turned around, looking as if he forgot something.

"Oh, yeah," he said, walking close to the salesman again.

Tom took a step back and tried to move when he saw the Indian's long arm come at him, but he was too slow and he felt the force of the fist as the knife stuck into his stomach. The Indian pulled it out and stepped back.

"If you tell anyone, I'll come back and kill you," he said, wiping the flat sides of the blade against a black leather vest hanging on a nearby rack.

When the chime announced the Indian's departure, Tom held his left hand over his wound and dialed the telephone for help with his other hand. He felt the warm pulse of blood through his fingers and he could tell that something was protruding from the gash. He was scared. He could feel his own blood leaving his body and then he felt another, warmer sensation in the crotch of his pants. Tom had wet himself.

A minute later his wife walked into the shop. She screamed when she found her husband of nine years laying on the floor in a widening circle of blood. He told her to hold something over the puncture until the ambulance arrived.

On the way to the hospital he told his wife that he loved her. She held his hand and spoke to him until he fainted while the medics tried to save his life.

Before Highmountain left the giftshop, he turned the OPEN sign over and switched off the lights. Outside on the street, he pulled the cash from his pocket and counted it while he walked. When he was done, he pushed the neat stack back into his pocket and walked on through the gray city light. The Indian didn't walk any faster than normal. It was as if he just came out of a bank and he was in no hurry.

After Philip had walked four blocks, a police car and an ambulance passed him heading downtown. Their lights and sirens were on, and they were in a hurry.

The flashing lights and the loud shreech from the vehicles reminded him what he had done. Suddenly it was real. Suddenly he was in trouble.

He picked up his pace and turned down other streets to put distance between himself and the giftshop. He had to get away from the city, and he was looking for a way out.

A building length ahead, Highmountain saw a silver taxi cab pull up and stop at a convenience store. It was a cold afternoon, and the driver went inside while leaving his car unlocked and idling.

"After turning himself into a woman to marry a man, Raven killed his husband late one night. The next day he told the dead man's kin to carry his husband's body far from the village and to bring food everyday while he mourned. Whenever someone came near that place, they heard Raven crying. He wasn't crying from sorrow, but from joy for having so easily tricked the villagers."

Chapter 6

Trooper Andrew Hudson left for work in the morning with only a cup of coffee and a bagel. Knowing that he'd be on the road for most of the day, his wife packed him a bag lunch. As she handed it to him she kissed him goodbye in their doorway.

"It's cold today, Andy," she warned as he walked to the warming car, nearly tripping on a blue, plastic sled. "Make sure you have your hat and gloves!" she yelled as he opened the door to his white patrol with the black and blue trooper's insignia on the side.

It was a very cold morning. The thermometer outside the window read thirty-two below, and the forecast called for lower temperatures with a slight wind from the north. It was so cold the car's tires were not entirely round, and they thumped with every rotation for the first few minutes as Trooper Hudson drove down the road. His log cabin vanished from sight after the first long turn.

The car was just beginning to warm up when he pulled into the station's parking lot and parked in his usual place. With the vehicle still idling, he went inside for his daily briefing and to refill his coffee mug. It was only a few dozen yards to the entrance, but even in the seconds it took to walk to the door, his ears were already beginning to hurt from the cold. It was still dark outside when the door closed hard behind him.

His colleague and friend, Trooper Jeff Stuart, smiled when he walked into the office.

"Morning, Andy," Jeff said. "Thanks for dropping off my boys last night. They told me they had a great time out on the lake," he continued.

Andrew Hudson loved fishing, and it was that love for fishing and hunting that led him to accept the post in this small rural town, some four hours from the nearest city. Yesterday afternoon he took his two boys and Stuart's two sons ice fishing on a nearby lake. It wasn't so cold yesterday. The temperature around noon was five below and the sun was shining. There was no wind, and they spent most of the afternoon snowmobiling and ice fishing. Although they caught only a couple nice trout, they still had a lot of fun. He had dropped off Jeff's kids around dinner time.

"They were great," Andy told his friend.

"Robert caught a nice one, and Mike lost a pretty good-sized trout," he continued, using his hands to show how long the one fish had been.

Andy read a few reports of the night's activities and refilled his ceramic car-mug. Then he made a few phone calls. Before he left the warmth of the building, he called his wife, Pam. They had been married almost eight years and were still madly in love. They met when they were both students at the university. He called her, like he did every day, to tell her that he loved her. He knew he wouldn't be off his shift until late, and he wanted her to tell the kids he loved them too and to be good at school. Andy smiled when he hung up the ivory-colored phone. He grabbed his mug and headed out the door to his idling patrol car.

It had snowed enough over the night to make the roads dangerous. Trooper Hudson spent much of the day patrolling the highway. Most of his stops were to help motorists whose vehicles had slid off the road. He issued a few citations for speeding, and even a couple tickets for inoperative headlights. All-in-all, it was a pretty normal day. He stopped at a lodge midway on his route to eat his sandwich and to have coffee. The lodge was a popular stop for motorists, especially for tourists in the summer. In the winter, snowmobilists from the city came here to play on weekends and to hunt in the backcountry.

The waitress was a pretty young girl around thirty, though she looked younger. Her name was Jacquie, and she smiled as she filled his mug from her glass container. The Trooper stopped at the lodge often and they always gave him free coffee while he talked about area happenings with the cooks and waitresses. Sometimes he talked with hunters returning from the field with their heavy piles of meat and antlers loaded on sleds or on the racks of four-wheelers.

"How's everything been today?" the waitress asked, noticing the black handle of his service automatic pistol sticking out only slightly from his unzipped dark blue jacket.

"Pretty regular day, Jacquie," he replied, noticing her beautiful eyes.

"The road's in pretty bad shape. What with the fresh snow and all. But, other than the cold, it's not too bad," he continued as he poured sugar and cream into his cup and stirred.

She looked at his face. Andy had dark hair. It was short, but not a crew cut. He had a clean-shaved face which always had a shadow, and he smiled often. Everyone liked Andy Hudson. He was well-known in the community. His oldest boy was in scouts and Andy volunteered as a den leader on Thursday nights. His wife was active in their children's school, and the family attended the local Baptist church regularly.

Jacquie smiled and put her free hand on his shoulder.

"Well," she said, "you just have a good day and don't drive too fast."

Outside the door was a thermometer within a big picture of a bottle with the words "Coka Cola" in white across the bottle and bright red background. When he came closer, Andy could see the numbers. On the far left side it could read as low as minus seventy. On the far right it could go up to ninety. The black needle was at thirty-five below. The sun would be going down in a few hours.

Inside the patrol car Hudson radioed the office to check in. It was procedure after his lunch break to call in and to receive updated reports, if any. Today he was told by Teresa, their detachment dispatcher, that a silver taxi cab had been stolen in the city at knife point by a Native man around thirty-five years old and about six feet tall. There were only three highways out of the city and all patrols were to be on the look-out for the car and driver. Andy wrote down the vehicle's description and license plate number on his note pad and he turned his car west, heading back to the station and home.

When he was about twenty-five miles west of the lodge, Hudson saw a silver car approaching. When it came close enough, he saw that it was a taxi cab, but he couldn't make out the license plate number. The trooper turned around and sped up behind the car. When at last he could read the license plate he radioed Dispatch and told them that he had located and identified the stolen car.

Then he turned on the car's lights and siren and sped up behind the taxi.

Instead of slowing down or pulling over, the driver sped up. The roads were iced-over in places, but the driver sped up to seventy miles per hour and then to eighty. Andy radioed in again and told Teresa that the car was evading him and that he was in pursuit.

Jeff Stuart, listening to the dispatch call, joined in the conversation.

"What's your twenty?" Jeff asked.

"About thirty-five miles west of town." responded Andy, watching the road. His knuckles were white in their tight grip on the steering wheel.

"At our current speed, you could set up a road block about halfway. We'll be there in about twenty, twenty-five minutes. If we don't crash first," Andy continued.

Trooper Stuart confirmed the plan with Dispatch and Trooper Stuart who set out with another officer to set up the blockade.

"See you in twenty minutes," Jeff said.

The sun was going down. It had already descended below the tops of a low hills, painting the thin horizon above orange and purple.

"It might be dark in fifteen minutes," Andy thought, as he followed the speeding taxi east on the highway, passing only one other car heading towards the city. One of its headlights was out.

"If I wasn't chasing this driver," Hudson thought, "I'd have gone after that other car."

"Lucky motorist," he said to himself, keeping his eye on the winding road ahead.

Up ahead was a sharp curve. From passing it earlier he knew that it was particularly icy on the other side. A yellow sign warned of the conditions, informing drivers to slow to thirty miles per hour. Normally he would have followed the sign's advice, but today he was pursuing a driver in a stolen taxi who didn't slow down, but instead increased speed.

Knowing how icy the road was, Hudson backed off the accelerator and pressed his brakes lightly. There was no hurry, no reason to risk his own safety. The blockade would be set up ahead and the driver would be stopped. Andy knew it was only a matter of time. The car in front of him gained ground as the distance between them increased.

When he came through the long curve he could see far ahead. The red tail lights of the silver cab looked small. Another motorist passed, going in the opposite direction. There were few cars on the road at this time of year, particularly on a weekday. Such a cold day could mean disaster if a vehicle broke down or even had a flat tire. Andy remembered last year's tragedy in which a family of three froze to death. One bitter February day, an elderly couple and their young granddaughter had taken off for a Sunday drive on a backcountry road rarely traveled during that time of year. They had told relatives that they were going south for the day, but decided after leaving the house to go north instead to an area where they picked berries in the fall.

After a few hours the temperature dropped drastically, but it was hard to notice inside their warm car. Sometime after they turned around to return home, their station wagon became stranded in a snowdrift about eighteen miles from the nearest house. They had no shovel to dig it out, and so they sat in the car until it finally ran out of gas. It was dark when the engine died, taking the heat with it and any chance that they would survive the night. The temperature outside was forty below. It was near zero when they began their trip that morning.

Although the family had lived in the region for many years, they didn't have cold weather gear with them on that day. When it was apparent that no other car would pass them, they decided to walk out after stamping the word "HELP" in big letters in the snow near the car. They were dressed poorly for the severe cold, especially the young girl. The night was harsh, even for a country of extremes. After they had walked maybe a quarter of the distance to a lodge, hypothermia seized their senses, gripping them so tightly that they quickly lost any feelings in their fingers and feet. Somewhere in the terrible night they began to feel warm, but it was only the lie of the suffering. Soon after, they lost their logic and left the road, walking out across open country in deep snow, shedding their hats, gloves, and jackets as they trudged on towards nowhere, following, perhaps, only the powdery light of the moon.

The next day Andy Hudson found the empty car. Several miles away he and Trooper Stuart found their frozen bodies, eyes open, and half naked several hundred yards apart. Apparently, after becoming so numb that they no longer felt cold or the pain in their limbs, the stranded party had begun to cast off their hats and gloves and jackets. It is a common phenomenon in hypothermia victims. Stumbling through the darkness like blind beggars, they had left the road and wandered out across open tundra.

Trooper Hudson tried to keep the silver car in sight. It was thirty-five below and the swaying spruce trees along the shoulder of the highway told him that the wind was up. The windchill was probably down to fifty below. Andy looked over and saw his hat and gloves on the seat beside him. He recalled what Pam had shouted to him that morning. He was thankful that he had remembered to bring them.

Hudson thought the car ahead must going ninety miles per hour.

"Surely," Andy thought, "he will get too far away. If it does, then the driver might turn around after seeing the blockade and come back this way."

All by himself he might not be able to stop the car from passing if it came at him from the opposite direction.

Andy pressed harder on the accelerator and the white and black patrol car jumped forward. Suddenly, ahead, he could see the red tail lights of the stolen taxi begin to fishtail. The lights went left and right. The taxi was spinning out of control at what Andy estimated to be eighty or ninety miles per hour. Hudson knew that the car was going to crash. He immediately slowed down so not as to wreck the patrol car.

Within seconds the car jumped from the highway and landed upside down about ten yards from the edge of the road in deep snow, just missing a thick spruce tree. Hudson maintained speed and reached for his hat. From his position, he could see a man crawl out from a window and crouch behind the front tire. Then the man began to run away from the road towards the forest. Even from the road, the trooper could see that the suspect had no hat or gloves, and no jacket. Andrew Hudson looked around. There was nothing but scraggly white spruce trees as far as he could see. In the far distance, about three miles, jagged mountains rose from the horizon and a low moon shone from just above a peak. Andy knew that the nearest house was twelve miles away.

There was no place fo the fleeing man to go. Andy wondered why the man was running. Where could he go? Grand theft auto and evasion wasn't worth freezing to death for in a night as terrible as this night was becoming, Andy thought.

By the time Andy's patrol car stopped, the figure was already well into the trees. Hudson opened the door, grabbed his gloves and flashlight in one hand and radioed dispatch with the other while standing outside the vehicle to better see the suspect. He was connected to the Troopers down the road who were only about five miles from base, some twenty-five minutes to this place. He told them that the suspect had crashed and was on foot and heading south. Mountains averaging seven to ten thousand feet in height, lay before him. There was no place to go, yet the shadowy figure kept moving slowly south as the moon became brighter until it became a large circle opposite a nearly indistinguishable horizon to the west.

Andrew Hudson left his warm car idling on the side of the road, its lights still flashing and walked out into the night. He pulled his gloves over his hands and pushed his fur hat lower onto his head, covering his ears which were already turning red from the cold and wind. He stepped from the plowed shoulder of the highway into the snowbank and immediately sank up to his waist. A few yards from the edge of the road, Andy found the snow was not as deep, perhaps five or six inches above his knees.

The trooper was six feet, four inches tall. During his two years of college he had played basketball. He was tall and lean, in good physical condition, but not powerful like a weightlifter or football jock. His long legs helped him press on through the snow. He was wearing long johns beneath his blue and black issue pants, and he was glad for them. He recalled that the report had stated that the suspect was shorter than he was, and he knew that the Indian was having a rougher time of it than he was. As he walked on, his black flashlight showing the tracks ahead, he thought about the Indian and how only a few miles back they had entered Indian Country. The local tribe controlled much of the lands in the region, and they had just entered the western-most boundary. In a way, this man in front of him had come home.

When he had followed the trail for several hundred yards, he came upon a rise where a long open area lay before him. There was less snow here and what there was was hard-packed. A strong wind swept across the field roughing the surface like sandpaper. The tracks vanished. When Andy had last seen them they were headed straight across towards the trees on the far side of the open field.

Here, in the night, on this ridge and field, a man could die in an hour without proper clothing or shelter. The suspect had neither, and once again Hudson wondered why this man would risk dying out here for theft.

"Perhaps he had been arrested before," the trooper thought. "Perhaps he was drunk or high and didn't know better."

Either way, Andy Hudson worried about the suspect as he pulled his parka's zipper up as high as it would go and walked out across the field, his flashlight low to the ground in search of footprints.

When he had gone halfway towards the treeline, Andy stopped, realizing that he was not so far behind the Indian that he could have reached the trees without having seen him. The trooper stood in the field, beneath a frond of new stars and the northern lights high above. He flashed his light on the far edge of the field in all directions, but found nothing. The wind masked any sounds the fleeing suspect might have made. Hudson turned and walked reluctantly back towards the road.

"In the morning a helicopter would scour the area and pick up on his tracks, if any," Andy thought. "That is, if he doesn't die first at the foot of some tree or freeze solid on some frozen lake or mountainside."

As he backtracked, Hudson began to wonder if the man might have tricked him, that even now the Indian was halfway back to the road. He recalled that his car was still running and unlocked. He started to walk faster, almost running through the now deep again snow. But, just as he made his way back into the dark forest, lit only by the moon, he saw something move. Whatever it was, it looked short, maybe three feet tall. The trooper ran forward, the wind and the rattling of trees covering the sound of his footsteps. When he was close enough, he saw the Indian crawling through the night and the snow and the freezing wind.

The figure stood and began to run. But he was only about ten yards away. The trooper drew his service pistol and aimed his flashlight at the back of the suspect.

"Stop running!" Andy yelled through the piercing wind. "You're under arrest! There's no place to go out here! Stop running and put your hands over your head!"

The Indian stood with his back to the trooper. His long black hair which fell far below his shoulders was blowing in the wind. He looked frozen. His pants were white and iced over. He had on no jacket or hat or gloves, and Andrew Hudson knew that he must be very cold, probably suffering from hypothermia.

"Stop running!" he yelled to the man again. "Put your hands behind your head!"

Still holding his flashlight and pistol, Andy Hudson walked up behind the suspect whose back was still to him.

"While Ganook was sleeping on his giant stone box, that crafty white Raven placed dog excrement beneath him. When Ganook awakened, Raven said 'Look. You have messed yourself.' When Ganook was outside washing himself, Raven lifted the heavy stone lid from the box and stole some of the fresh water."

Chapter 7

The flashing lights were closer now. The patrol car had been gaining for the last few miles, and Philip Highmountain knew it would be upon him soon. He pressed the accelerator to the floor, running the needle up past ninety. Too fast on these icy roads, but he had to lose the trooper. The scraggly spruce trees passed by him faster now, but the red and blue lights were still coming. Soon they would fill his rear view mirror until there would be nothing left of dusk but blinding lights and the penetrating scream of siren.

The Indian reached down with his right hand and felt around for a bottle on the seat beside him. When he found it, he twisted the cap and swallowed hard for a long time until it was empty. Then he let it drop to the floor, clinking against the other half dozen beer bottles which lay there among cassettes and two spent packs of cigarettes.

He saw the knife lying on the seat beside the last full bottle. He picked it up and looked at it. It was a nice knife, an expensive one. The blade wasn't all that long, but the handle was handsome, and it had a good heft and balance.

The Indian sat it back on the seat and focused on the road.

Just ahead, before a sharp turn, a yellow sign warned of slippery road conditions. He saw it only for a second, little time for warning. But there was no turning back. No time for safety. This could be his opportunity to make some headway, to leave the trooper behind.

Highmountain hadn't driven in a long time, and he wasn't good at it. He never had his own vehicle, not even the one he used when he made love to Sue. He never owned his own car and he never really wanted one. Not since what happened to his friend's baby.

"It must have been when he was in his late teens, almost nineteen," the Indian thought.

A bunch a friends from school got together at a girl named Mary's house. Her parents were gone for the weekend and she had the house to herself. And her friends. She had just finished high school and had her baby, who must have been two months old when it happened. Mary didn't know who the father was, and her parents let the two stay at their house since she had no job or money.

It was a sunny day when the party began late in the afternoon. It was warm and there was no wind. Mary took her baby outside in his little infant carrier and placed it behind her car so that he could sleep in the shade. Hours later the beer ran out, and her friends pitched in the money to buy more. Half drunk, Mary started her old four door car, looked in the rear window to see if she was blocked in by her friend's cars and trucks, and then she backed out of her driveway.

She didn't think much about the bump under her right tires until she had backed clean out of her driveway, and she could see the blood splattered all over the gravel and the mangled plastic carrier.

Highmountain forcibly brushed away the memory, and held his breath rounding the bend. Just as he came out of the long curve, the car began to swerve, turning sideways. It was out of control, turning first one way and then the other on the narrow road. It had been years since he had driven a car, and it only made matters worse when he smashed his foot onto the brakes. There was no stopping the spin. The needle still read near ninety as the car spun dizzily out of the Indian's control. But the flashing lights were farther behind now.

The car spun its way down the middle of the road until finally it found its way to the shoulder, and beyond. Philip Highmountain and the silver car left the icy road together and plunged over an embankment, landing nose-first and flipping over in a storm of snow and steam rising from the overheated engine. The inflated air bag kept him from flying through the windshield, which surely would have killed him. Without the bag, his body would have been mangled, most likely suffering smashed ribs and bones, and he would have bled out upon the dash and windshield.

Philip looked back towards the road. The lights were still far away and small. He pushed against the driver's door, but it wouldn't open. Most of the door lay buried in snow. The Indian kicked out the side window and pulled himself from the wreck, cutting his left hand on the jagged edge that remained. He didn't have on his jacket and he could feel the cold.

"It must be thirty below," he thought.

Scrambling to his feet Highmountain looked for the trooper, whose slowing car was almost to where the taxi's tracks left the highway.

Philip turned and ran towards the forest. The waist deep snow slowed him, but it would slow the trooper as well. He ran away from the road, away from the law. He ran away from the stolen taxi cab and, he hoped, away from incarceration. No one knew who was driving the stolen taxi or who had robbed the furrier. Not yet at least. If he could only get away, no one would come looking for him. They wouldn't knock on Philip Highmountain's door. He would get past this night and that would be the end of it.

He saw the sun low on the sharp horizon, and he knew that it would be dark soon. If he could only put some distance between himself and the trooper, he might still escape. Ignoring his anxiety and fear, Philip pushed on towards the wilderness. His hand was still bleeding and as he ran he held his good hand tight against the wound.

The deep snow slowed him more than he thought. He must have run only fifty yards before stopping to catch his breath. He turned and saw the trooper for the first time. The man was standing beside the open door of his patrol car with a radio in one hand. His dark blue parka looked almost black in the distance. He looked taller than the Indian, but thinner. Not as powerful. Highmountain turned away and again began to push through the deep snow. After about seventy yards, he turned to see the lawman already gaining on him, his longer legs moving him through the snow more easily. The sound of a passing car on the highway told him that he was not yet far enough from the road.

But he was already very cold and he began to shiver.

"Shit. It must be forty below," he thought. "Colder perhaps."

"And it will be even colder after the sun sets," he thought, looking at the low sun and partially cloudy sky.

His pant legs were wet from snow and sweat. They would freeze stiff if he rested too long. He had to keep moving. He had no jacket or hat or gloves. He figured he would freeze out here and die among the trees and snow. The last milepost had told him that it was more than thirty miles to the next town. Too far to travel on foot in winter without cold weather gear. He knew he would die in the dark of this forest if he didn't get back to the highway soon.

The trail came upon a small rise where the wind and sun had hardened the snow to a crust. His tracks were barely distinguishable in the failing light, and in minutes the breeze would erase what little existed of his tracks. Ahead, he saw a tree which was a little fuller than the ones around it. Beyond it lay a field or a frozen pond. It was hard to tell them apart in winter. He ran toward the spruce tree. He would hide beneath its boughs until the trooper, in his warm winter clothes passed, looking for him out across the wind-swept plain. He would wait and then backtrack to the road to take the trooper's car which even now was idling, its interior warm as the glow of its dashboard lights.

Philip remembered how as a boy he used to sleep in his father's Chevy on long road trips. He would sleep in the back seat of the green Nova which smelled like the stale empty beer bottles usually rattling around on the passenger's side floor. When there became too many bottles, they were tossed back to where the boy slept where they would fall to the floor there and clink each time the car hit a bump or took a sharp turn. The car was warm, and the glowing green dashboard lights made it somehow even warmer. He remembered how safe he felt then, lying on the vinyl back seat under his torn and patched jacket with his head propped against the vinyl-covered door. His father, who was drunk most of the time, couldn't beat Philip while he was driving. The backseat of that car was one of the safest places in his childhood. It could have been sixty below outside, but the car was always warm and country music was always played loudly on the radio. His dad had eight track tapes scattered on the seat beside him or on the floor. Between the music and the clinking beer bottles, Philip would sleep and dream. But out here tonight among the wind and rising moon it was of little consolation.

    He crept close beneath the tree's boughs and huddled there, protected momentarily from the slight wind turning his wet bluejeans into ice. The Indian watched as a dark figure ran across the packed snow, a flashlight illuminating his way. Highmountain saw that it was the trooper. The man ran out across the field or frozen pond, but then he stopped suddenly and stood still, his small circle of light sweeping the ground like a broom. Snow, driven by wind, drifted across the trooper's feet like a white snake. Drifts wound around his feet, up his legs, and then, almost as if angry, uncoiled and released their victim, sliding along the crusted surface sideways in search of another solitary prey. Philip watched as the man looked at the ground, then ahead.

Highmountain, crouched in the tree's darkness, holding his breath. He waited in the shadow and shivered uncontrollably.

"It was too far to the other edge of the field," he thought. "He knows I couldn't have covered that distance so quickly."

From where he sat, he could see the trooper looking around him, thinking about the events which had brought him to this place.

"He knows I couldn't be so far ahead," the Indian thought, his brown eyes staring through spruce boughs.

The trooper must have figured that even now the suspect was behind him, maybe halfway to the idling patrol car. Perhaps he would take the car and escape, leaving the trooper alone on the highway.

In the twilight of late dusk, the tall lawman turned and walked back towards the treeline. He walked slowly and deliberately, using his flashlight to illuminate the snow just ahead of him. In a few minutes he would be close to the spruce tree, and he would see the Indian huddled beneath its cover, freezing in his frozen pants and shoes and holding his wounded hand under an armpit for warmth.

Highmountain reached into his right pocket for his lighter, but it had fallen out when the taxi cab flipped. He couldn't build a fire anyhow, not with the trooper so close. He put both hands under his armpits and sat facing the horizon, watching stars rise for their long journey into night. He sat and waited as the tall dark figure approached.

"He'll find me here and arrest me, and they'll put me in prison again," Philip thought.

It was only yesterday morning the Indian had been released from prison after more than three years. He had spent almost half of his life imprisoned for one crime or another. Twelve years in all. He remembered the guards joking about seeing him again. One of the guards grabbed himself between the legs and blew the Indian a kiss goodbye after the last steel door slammed shut and locked with a heavy clank.

"We'll see you again real soon!" the guard had yelled through the bars as he turned and went back to work, laughing so loud that he could be heard through an open window outside on the sidewalk leading to the gate.

"But they wouldn't," he promised himself. "Not in this lifetime. Not so soon."

Philip felt a sudden surge of anxiety and anticipation.

Now the lawman was almost upon him. Highmountain crawled out from under the spruce tree. His hands hurt badly from the cold, but he could still feel them and that was a good thing. He crawled past another tree and behind a drift, thrusting his hands deep into the snow which bit into them like wolves each time he pushed them in. When he was far enough away, he stood up and ran back towards the road. His legs were numb, and he couldn't feel his ears or cheeks.

He hadn't gone two dozen steps when he heard a voice calling to him through the thin cold air. It was the first time he had heard the man's voice, and it surprised him somehow. He didn't know why it surprised him, but it did. Perhaps it was too calm. Perhaps he expected the voice to be shaky and nervous, nearly frozen like his own. But the words were clear and closer than he thought. He turned and saw the trooper almost upon him. The man had a long black flashlight in one hand and a handgun in the other. He was telling him to stop running, that there was no place to go.

Philip Highmountain, out of jail only a day, drunk and cold and tired, stopped and let out a long sigh. His powerful shoulders fell forward in resignation. His pants felt like a blocks of ice against his legs, and he could no longer feel his right hand at all.

"At least I won't freeze to death out here in the middle of nowhere," he thought.

Far ahead through the forest, Philip Highmountain could see the small faint lights of the patrol car perhaps two hundred yards away.

As he raised his arms above his head, his long black hair blew wildly in the night wind. Through the darkness, a raven called out to his brethren and was answered from afar.

"Because Raven wasn't a very good fisherman, he decided to trick Seagull and Crane. He told each of them that the other wanted to fight. Then he told Seagull to kick Crane in the chest. When he did, Crane spat out the big herring he had just swallowed, and Raven flew away laughing at the two birds."

Chapter 8

Somewhere in the world, the sun was warm and shining, and people were resting on white sand beaches with an umbrelled cocktail in one hand and their lover's hand in the other. But in this forest tonight there was only loneliness, cold, and the dark white reflection of moon as it fell between scraggly trees onto a fabric of snow which lay outstretched like bones below. A slant wind broke night's plentiful solitude. Only the shadows of two men moving across the landscape broke the stillness, suggesting that this place was somehow alive.

A dark figure, standing still, his black hair loose and long, slowly raised his arms above his head.

"I said turn around!" the Trooper called, his voice just rising above the sound of wind cracking branches in its teeth.

But the other man didn't move. Andy wondered if the suspect had a weapon. He didn't want to get too close until he was certain.

"Turn around now! You're under arrest," he yelled again.

The Trooper began to think maybe the man was dead. Maybe he froze stiff standing there. Maybe he was deaf. After another minute passed he walked through the snow closer to the man and shone his flashlight up and down the figure's back, searching for any obvious presence of weapons. When he couldn't find anything, he spoke to the Indian again, this time he didn't have to yell so loudly.

"I'm a State Trooper. You're under arrest for grand theft auto and evasion. I'm going to ask you to turn around. Then I'm going to handcuff you one hand at a time. Then we'll walk back to my warm car and I'll take you into town."

The figure stood still. There was no response. It was as if he hadn't heard him at all.

"Do you understand what I have said?" asked Trooper Hudson, his service pistol still in his right hand.

The man nodded slightly. Slowly he began to turn around to face the trooper, his hands still behind his head.

Finally, they were face to face. Only about ten feet separated them. The Trooper saw how poorly the man was dressed. He had no hat or gloves. He had on only a flannel shirt and denim jeans with a hole on one knee.

There was blood on his cuffs and on the front of his shirt. From where he stood, Andy could see the cut on the Indian's hand.

"This man must be freezing to death," Andy thought.

"Are you alright?" he asked the Indian who nodded that he was not.

"What's your name?" he asked, looking into the other man's eyes.

"Highmountain," the man said, almost too softly to hear.

"Ok, Highmountain. Now listen to me carefully and we can get this over with and go back to my warm car," Andy said, trying to keep a friendly tone. He needed to diffuse the situation and for the suspect to believe that everything would be alright.

"Do you have any weapons on you? Any guns or knives? He flashed his light up and down the front of the man looking for signs of weapons.

The Indian was shaking badly, but he answered.

"No," he said, looking past the trooper, almost through him as if he wasn't really there. As if somehow hypothermia had conjured up this ghost standing before him.

"Lower your right hand and place it behind your back," Andrew said in a calm voice. He wanted the man to know that he was in control.

The Indian lowered his right arm slowly. It was obvious that he couldn't quite control its movement.

Trooper Hudson placed his handgun back into its holster, leaving the thumbsnap off. Then he came closer to the man and placed his right hand in a steel cuff and quickly locked it tight. He felt relieved that the man was not resisting any longer.

They were close now. Maybe only two feet apart.

Andy spoke again.

"Now I want you to do the same thing with your other hand. I want you to put it behind your back, too. Ok?"

Highmountain began to lower his arm just as he had done with the first one. But when it was almost all the way down, he made a fist and spun around as hard as he could, throwing his arm up and out. The fist smashed against the Trooper's head. The impact made him fall off balance, dropping to one knee in the deep snow. His flashlight fell from his hand, its light shining on the Indian. Andy tried to stand up, but before he could Highmountain kicked him high on his chest just below his neck, knocking him onto his back. For a moment he could see the stars and clouds beginning to cover the acetylene-white moon.

He lay there for only a few seconds, but it felt good. Sometimes in the fall and early winter he lay with his wife and children in the field behind their cabin to watch the stars. The nights were spectacular and they would lie in a row upon pads and sleeping bags and watch the sky and talk for hours. He wondered what they were doing now.

Just then the Indian jumped on him and Andy could feel the weight upon him. He struggled to his side, and with one arm beneath him he tried to lift himself to where he could get a knee under his body.

Suddenly, the weight was off of him and the trooper stood up to face the man who had attacked him. The Indian had his gun in two hands and was pointing it at him from only a few feet. It was too easy, and Hudson was mad at himself for his mistake. He had been trained at the academy against such an event, and he remembered the lessons well. He should have kept his distance, at least twice the distance. He stood too close because the wind was too loud. He should have had the suspect lie face down with his face in the snow. But he took pity on the freezing Indian, and now he had the gun and it was pointed at his chest from only five or six feet away.

"I'm not goin' back, man! I'm not gonna. Don't follow me," the Indian said as he backed away, making the distance between them wider.

Hudson said nothing, but watched as the man turned and walked away with his pistol towards his car on the highway. It was darker now that the moon was half-engulfed in clouds. Even the dim stars were barely visible above the glacial earth.

When he could no longer see Highmountain, Andrew grabbed his flashlight and followed the trail, almost running through the night and snow. When he thought he had was close enough, the trooper turned the light off so that the Indian wouldn't see that he was already being followed.

Halfway to the car Andy could see the suspect silhouetted against the flashing red and blue lights from the car beyond him. They weren't that far apart, but the wind was still masking sounds and the Indian was night-blind from looking at the lights ahead. When he turned, Highmountain saw nothing but a dark and cold forest.

"It was a lonely place," he thought. "It would be a cold place to die."

The trooper crouched when he saw the man turn around. But after a few seconds the Indian turned again and threw something. Even from the distance Andy could see its shape. It was his pistol. The Indian had thrown the gun into the snow and and began to walk the last hundred yards to the warm, idling patrol car.

Now the Trooper ran the trail which was broke from where the two men had walked before on their way to the open field. The man ahead still heard only the savage wind and kept his walking pace. In a minute the Trooper was upon the man and he jumped with his arms outstretched to grab around the Indian's waist when they collided.

The momentum threw both men hard into the snow and they wrestled there, eaching trying to push the other away. The Indian hit the trooper across the face twice, the steel cuff on his right hand cutting into Hudson's face, spilling blood upon his jacket and onto the crushed snow beneath them.

Highmountain turned and ran towards the car. But before he covered even a dozen steps, the trooper was on him again, his longer legs and warmer muscles covering the distance quickly. They fought again. This time both men landed punches on the other. But always the Indian was trying to break free. Once, Hudson shoved his assailant into a spruce tree and the low branches scraped his face, almost cutting the Indian's left eye.

Only a few minutes passed, but they seemed like forever. All the while Andy kept thinking about how the other trooper's were miles down the road. They wouldn't be here for five or ten minutes. Maybe longer. He had to keep the Indian away from his car just a few more minutes.

Highmountain grabbed on to the trooper's parka and Hudson held on to the Indian's flannel shirt tight-fisted. Their heads were butting as both men tried to widen their stance, making it harder to be thrown off balance. Hudson made a move first. He dropped quickly and unexpectedly to the small of his back, placed both feet against the Indian's stomach, and with a rolling motion sent the suspect flying onto his back hard. The snow cushioned the fall which would have normally knocked the air from his lungs.

Scrambling to their feet they were soon upon each other back on the ground. Both men were tired now, and Andy took the opportunity to speak .

"Listen. Two more Trooper's will be here any minute. They're gonna shoot you if they see us fighting like this. Understand?" he asked, barely able to catch his breath.

Instead of replying, the Indian fought harder. He punched the trooper twice in the side and then he broke free and tried to stand up.

"I'm not going back to jail, man," he said, as he turned and looked down at Hudson who grabbed one of his pant legs. Highmountain tried to pull away. His green flannel shirt was torn and covered with both mens' blood. But Andy held on tight, and the Indian couldn't break free. He turned around and kicked at Hudson's face, but the trooper moved his head and grabbed the man's foot. Then he stood up, spilling the Indian onto the snow. Hudson jumped onto the man and they wrestled again.

"Look!" he yelled into Highmountain's face. "They're gonna be here any minute. Do you understand that? You need to stop now."

The man didn't respond this time as he struggled to get loose.

Finally, the Indian was able to get on top, and he pressed the trooper's face down into the snow. The red and blue lights lit the tops of trees. The temperature was even lower now than it had been when the silver taxi first crashed. The snow stung the trooper's flesh, and the moon was covered entirely by clouds now. His hands were numb.

The Indian put all his weight across the Trooper's back so that one of Hudson's arms was pinned behind his back and the other was pinned beneath him. He tried to escape, but he couldn't. He could feel the Indian's hand when it came across his face, feeling around for his mouth and nose, trying to shut off his air, trying to suffocate him.

For the first time Andrew Hudson was afraid. All during the chase and ensuing fight he had thought mostly for the suspect's safety. Now he thought of his own. He was in a dangerous situation and he was angry that he had not been more careful.

"He would never make that mistake again," he promsed himself.

He knew what his commander would say, and he knew that he was going to be in a lot of trouble for letting this suspect take possession of his weapon. He redoubled his effort, trying hard to shake loose the Indian, but no matter how hard he tried, the man was still upon him, and his arms were still pinned uselessly beneath him.

When the hand found his mouth, Hudson struggled as hard as he could against the weight and he screamed, but the sound was muffled in the deep snow. There was no one else to hear anyhow, only a Raven who had landed atop a tree nearby, interested perhaps only by the strange sounds invading his otherwise peaceful home. Although he tried as hard as he could, Hudson couldn't dislodge the man who was killing him. He turned his head from side to side, and tried to hold his breath. He tried to pull his one arm free from beneath him. All the while, his lungs burned. He had gone diving several times on vacation, and he knew how it felt when the air began to run out while he was still deep beneath the surface. He felt that way now. He felt the strong brown hand across his face and the great weight upon him.

As he began to lose consciousness, Andrew Hudson thought about his wife. He had made love to her this morning in the their warm bed with heavy quilts and soft white sheets. In his mind, he reached out to pull her close as he had done for nine years. They kissed and she pulled away until only their fingers touched. Then there was nothing, as darkness consumed his vision, taking his every thought with it.

"After Raven challenged Brown Bear to a sliding contest, he quickly flew to the bottom of the slope and placed his long hunting knife such that its sharp blade pointed straight out. When Brown Bear slid down the hill first, he was killed by the knife and Raven started eating him as soon as he was dead."

Chapter 9

The Raven which had been sitting nearby on a spindly spruce tree suddenly lifted into the air, his black body rising into the night sky. He cawed loudly to the world, screeching profanities. Then, as mysteriously as he appeared, he vanished into the slice of light which curved like a yolk into a horizon as thin as the edge of a knife.

Highmountain held the man tight against his body. The Indian's arms and legs were tense as coils. He held his right hand tight across the trooper's mouth and nose and pressed the other man's head deep into the snow with his left hand. All around were signs of their struggle. One trail led to the car and the other back into the forest. He looked both ways and then back down before him. Then he closed his eyes and waited. One minute. Two minutes. He remembered hunting with his uncle when he was young. They used to take a snowmachine upriver to a slough were rabbits were abundant. It was midwinter and the river ice was thick. On the way they would pass fish traps set beneath the ice and snow.

Philip recalled one of those days. He carried a single shot twenty-two rifle. It was an old and battered thing, and his name was carved into the stock. The bolt always came out if he pulled back too hard, and the front sight had been lost years earlier. His father had welded a cut nail onto the barrel's end as a sight, and he used a length of yellow nylon rope as a sling. But it was accurate. He used it to hunt birds and rabbits. Once, he remembered, he had even shot a fox from about fifty yards.

His uncle and he hunted all day in the sunshine, the brilliant snow blinding them when they looked out across the wide river. That afternoon they had killed maybe a dozen rabbits and four or five grouse. They never died right away. To save bullets he would take the small animals, their eyes wide in fear and pain, and twist their necks sharply until their tiny feet stopped clawing at his wrists. When they were still, he tossed them into a canvas bag on their sled and they turned homeward, following their tracks into sunset.

Highmountain felt the same way now. There was something indescribable about what he was doing. When a small animal was bleeding and alive, there was a need to kill it quickly. Not so much to end its pain, perhaps, but more a need to end the feeling of guilt inside. Death was a part of life, and he had been taught that since childhood.

But here, in this lonely place, he felt neither a sense to end the pain of this animal, nor a desire to quickly end his own guilt. This was different. He had never before experienced the sheer power of this moment, the thrill.

He looked down at the still figure beneath him, saw his head and lazy neck. How easy, he thought, it would be to turn it sharp like a grouse's tiny skull and hear that small snap of bone he had heard so many times in his life. The Indian took the head in both hands. It was heavy and it moved easily from side to side. He was about to twist it as fast and hard as he could, when his attention was caught by a sound.

Highmountain looked up from atop the dead trooper's corpse. A car had stopped and he could see its red and blue lights. He rolled off the body and lay beside it, his head just above the man's shoulder. A moment later he could see a trooper with a flashlight standing on the road looking out across the snow into the woods. The man wasn't that far away, maybe sixty or seventy yards at most, but small trees and a bush hid him from the light.

Staying low, the Indian pulled the parka from the trooper and put it on himself. The gloves and hat had been lost back where they had first fought. Highmountain reached down and unlaced the dead trooper's black boots and pulled them from his feet. Then he rolled down the socks and slipped them over his hands. They were wool and they would keep him warm. He looked around for the pistol which he had thrown into the snow, but he knew it wouldn't be found until spring when the deep snow reluctantly gave way to small berry plants and wild flowers.

There were no other weapons on the trooper's belt.

Now the light was moving away from the road towards him. The trooper had found the trail. Philip crawled away from the still body and hid behind a tree. He knew that he couldn't stay there long. The trooper would find him in a minute, see what he had done, and shoot him on sight. He looked around and decided on a direction where more trees would offer protection. He crouched and forced his way through the deep snow, tripping once on a log beneath him.

When he came to the next tree, he huddled under it and turned to see the other trooper who was already to the body. From where he hid he could see the man bent over, his hand on the other man's neck. The Indian watched as the trooper stood up, shone his light around him. Only one path led away from the scene and in an instant the trooper would be on his trail, his flashlight searching the ground like a bloodhound.

What had been the hunter was now the rabbit again.

Highmountain raised himself up and ran. He heard the man behind him yelling, but he kept running without looking behind. The voice called out again and was followed by gunfire, its report shattering the night. Even the moon seemed to wake up as clouds released it and darkness was lifted again. Now the trooper's blood was bright red on the snow around where the body lay. Somehow the bright moonlight made the scene more real, the murder more horrific.

Just then another car pulled up. A man jumped out, and Philip could hear the door slam clearly. Then a powerful spotlight began searching the highway's edge near where trees began to build a forest, its light pouring through branches and brush like a stream, illuminating drifts and small rises until it found the other trooper who waved his own light back towards the cars. The Indian could hear their muffled radio talk, but he couldn't make out what they were saying.

While he fought and killed the trooper his body had warmed. The blood in his veins had surged during their struggle, and he was sweating in the parka with its too long sleeves. But now his ears were numb again. He held his sock-covered hands over them and began to run again. After he had run a ways he came upon a stream. It was as wide as a road lane. Too far to jump across. The cold spell had set in quickly, and the water was still open in places. Steam rose into the night where the savage air touched water.

The Indian ran alongside the creek, knowing it would be too dangerous to cross the thin ice. If he fell through, the current might pull him beneath the ice like it had done his cousin, Charley. Philip was thirteen when it happened. Charley was twelve. They had gone away from the village on snowmachines to play for the day. It was early spring and the snow was almost gone. It was a beautiful day when they came upon a small stream only about a dozen feet across, very much like this one. The ice was so clear that they could see to the bottom. Both boys knew that it was deep and that it ran between two small lakes. It was as much as seven to ten feet deep in places. They came here with their families in the fall to hunt moose and pick berries, and they knew the place well.

Philip was the first to cross. He made a wide circle, turned the machine towards the icy surface and gunned the throttle. He must have hit the creek at forty miles an hour. Where he crossed the ice fractured, its pattern a spider web shining in sunlight. When he was on the other side, Philip turned and waited for his uncle's son. They had grown up together in their small village. Everyone was somehow related to everyone else. That's the way things were back then. There was only a few white people around, and most of them were teachers.

Philip waved at Charley, motioning him to try it himself.

"It's ok!" he yelled across to his cousin.

Charley pulled the starter rope, sat up high on the machine to better see through the cracked and duct-taped windshield, and gunned the throttle. But instead of gliding over the creek as Philip had done, his machine plunged through the ice, both boy and machine disappearing in a splash and the sound of ice shattering. When Charley's head appeared, Highmountain laughed.

"Hell, boy! Don't you know better than to cross thin ice? Damn, that's got to hurt like hell," he yelled as he walked up to the edge of the creek, looking for a stick to use to pull his cousin from the freezing water.

Charley tried to hold his place but the current was stronger than it looked. It pushed him against the thin sheet of river ice.

"Help me, Phil!" Charley screamed to his taller cousin, feeling the current yanking at his legs, trying to pull him under.

Highmountain kept laughing and looking on the ground for a stick.

"Your dad's gonna kill you and your momma's gonna tan your ass when you get home," Philip said, still looking around for something to use.

When he finally broke a spruce bough off a tree, he turned and saw his cousin go under. He ran as close as he could, but Charley didn't come up.

"Charley!" he yelled.

Highmountain looked around until he saw his cousin being pulled downriver beneath the ice. He was alive and pounding at the ice above him frantically. His eyes were wide and they followed Philip's movements in terror as he ran along the edge. All the while Charley pounded at the ice, clear as a window.

Philip took a chance, running out onto the ice, just above his cousin. He kicked at the surface with his boot. He kicked as hard as he could and he smacked the stick against the ice which was thicker here. Try as he could, though, he could not fracture the surface. Highmountain ran above his cousin for more than a minute around a bend until he saw Charley gulp for air. Then his body stopped flailing, his eyes closed, and his limp body floated downstream only inches away beneath a polished mirror of ice.

As his cousin's body disappeared around a bend, Highmountain stood in the middle of the creek alone, his eyes full of tears, his hands and legs trembling. He looked around for help, but there was no one around for miles. Nothing moved except a dried leaf blown across the snow, and a small boy's body flowing under clear ice downriver where it would sink beneath a small lake and his family would find what remained of his corpse in the late spring more than a month later.

In the twenty or so years since that day Philip had never forgotten the way his cousin looked at him. It haunted his dreams. There were many nights in prison when Philip woke up screaming for his cousin who drowned that spring in childhood. Highmountain's own drowning was much slower, lasting many years.

A wind picked up and blew snow hard against his face. The ice crystals were stiff and they felt like tiny needles driven into his eyes. Philip squinted and put the thought of Charley behind, like the dead trooper's body.

The Indian ran across the glacial earth, his heart pounding and his ears and legs numb. His pant legs were frozen again, and his toes felt like someone was smashing them with a hammer. He could see the trooper running behind him. To his left, through a bank of trees, he could see the patrol car moving along the road in the same direction. The stream paralleled the road for nearly a mile. The patrol car was less than a hundred yards away, and it would not be further away for the next mile. The spotlight flooded him as he ran, his moon shadow falling at his feet before him, as if it too was running away from something.

Thirty miles down the highway, the river of his youth flowed slowly past villages, gathering shadows from the darkness, as it followed its course, sometimes beneath thick and brittle ice, through the frozen, starry night.

"After deceiving the young human woman into marrying him, Raven took her to his house. The woman sniffed the air and said to her new husband, 'It smells like Raven's asshole in here.' Raven told her to stop complaining and flew away. He didn't stay married long."

Chapter 10

Jeff Stuart could see the flashing lights of patrol car a half mile away. He was several minutes ahead of the other trooper's car which had to stop for fuel on the way. It had been too long since anyone had last heard from Hudson, and he was worried. He thought maybe Andy was just having radio trouble. There were places on the highway where reception was lost behind sharp turns pressed against steep bluffs cut into the mountains. He hoped he was right about the radio as he stopped his vehicle beside Hudson's, even though this area was flat and he usually got fine reception on this part of the road.

The other car was empty, but its engine was still running, and its headlights were aimed just right of a car which was upside down in deep snow a dozen or so yards from the icy road.

Stuart opened his door and stood outside. It was cold. He reached back inside for his hat and gloves, turned on the searchlight and aimed its beam at the wreck, searching for signs of his friend and the suspect. The car matched the report's description, but there was no sign of his colleague or the suspect.

"Andy!" he yelled several times.

It was windy enough that Jeff knew his voice wouldn't travel far.

He moved the light around until he found tracks leading into the forest. He looked back up the highway where he saw the other patrol car's tiny headlights and flashing lights coming over a far ridge several miles up the road.

"It'll be here in a couple minutes," he thought, as he pulled his flashlight from its stand and headed into the dark woods where tips of spruce swayed in the wind and clouds hiding the moon began to break up.

He walked cautiously, listening for voices ahead. Although the crime report had stated that only one man, an Indian, had stolen the taxi at knife point, he could not be certain that he was now alone.

When Stuart was a ways into the forest he saw something ahead. It was too dark to clearly see what it was, so the trooper moved closer until he saw that it was a body lying face down in the snow. He flashed his light upon it as he approached. He was relieved when he saw that it wasn't wearing a trooper's dark blue parka.

"It must be the suspect," he thought, looking around for Andy.

Stuart reached down to roll the man over to check for a pulse, but it was too heavy to turn him in the deep snow with one hand. He set his flashlight down on the crushed trail and rolled the body over.

Just then the clouds released a bone-white moon and its light shone on the man's face.

It was Hudson.

Stuart grabbed his flashlight and held it close to the man's face.

"Holy shit!" he said aloud.

He moved the light up and down Hudson's body. His parka was missing and even his boots and socks had been removed. Jeff pulled off his right glove with his teeth and touched Andy's neck, feeling for a pulse. He crouched there like that for half a minute or longer. All the while he flashed his light up and down the trail. When he could find no pulse, he stood up, pulled the thumb strap off his holster, and flashed his light up the trail.

Just then the other patrol car arrived. Stuart reached into his parka, took out his handheld radio, and spoke to the other trooper still inside his vehicle.

"God damn it, J. D., it's Andy. He's dead," His voice was nervous and shaken.

While the two men spoke, Jeff looked around, using his light to uncover every tree, bush, or drift. His heart was pounding and he had a headache.

Suddenly, a figure burst out from beneath a small tree maybe thirty yards to his right. Jeff trained his light on the shadow, but it was too far to make clear.

"Stop!" he yelled at the figure. The man kept running. Then he yelled again and fired his weapon into the air, the flash lighting a small circle around him.

"He's heading east," Jeff told the other trooper who was still inside his vehicle.

J. D. Jones, a rookie who had lived in the region for most of his life, radioed back.

"Hey, Jeff. Moose Creek runs parallel to the road here for a mile or so. It's just behind you a little ways," he continued. "It's spring-fed. He's not gonna be able to cross it."

"So?" asked Stuart.

"If you follow him and I get ahead of you, there'll be no place for him to go," the rookie continued.

Jeff agreed. He replaced the radio into his jacket, pulled up his zipper, and then he walked out into the night after the man who had killed a fellow officer, and his friend. Hudson was the first trooper to die in the line of duty in this state for almost fifteen years. No trooper had ever been killed at this post.

Stuart was angry, and he gripped his stainless steel automatic tight, hoping that he'd have to shoot the bastard.

Their job was tough out here, but generally not too dangerous. Most of their incidents involved drunk drivers, hunting and boating accidents, and the occasional poaching. There was a good deal of assault in the Indian villages, mostly domestic, but there was no drugs or gangs.

The snow reflected the moon's shine so much that Jeff could see without his maglite. Although the suspect had to plow his way through deep snow, Jeff stepped into the holes he made and was able to travel easier. Not far ahead he could see the back of the suspect, weaving around trees and deadfalls. To his left he could see the other trooper driving slowly, his searchlight illuminating the forest.

A snowshoe rabbit suddenly burst out from behind a small bush nearby. The unexpected movement, so close, surprised him.

"Within a quarter mile or less, the creek will turn towards the highway and cross beneath a the bridge," the trooper thought. "There'll be no place to go, and this murderer will be caught."

Stuart thought about this, but he also thought about his dead friend lying alone in the snow behind him. He was determined to catch this man, and as he walked, he checked his weapon, making certain that there was a round in the chamber. He was ready for anything.

After a few minutes the trooper could see the trail change. It was heading left. The suspect was moving towards the highway.

"It won't be long now," Jeff thought, as he pulled out his radio from inside his parka, slipping his pistol back into its holster momentarily.

"J.D., can you hear me?" he asked quietly.

"Ya, Jeff. Go ahead."

"Listen. The trail's turning towards you. Go on ahead up to the bridge and turn off your engine and lights and wait for him to cross," he said, almost tripping on a log or rock under the snow.

"Affirmative," replied Trooper Jones, turning off the searchlight and speeding ahead to set up an ambush.

Jeff turned down the radio's volume and placed it inside his pocket so that he could get to it in a hurry if he needed it. Then he pulled out his service automatic and continued his walk across a glacial earth. His feet were wet and cold from snow which had worked down into his boots. His cheeks were frozen and moisture from his eyes sometimes froze his eyelashes shut. It was so cold outside that the air hurt when he breathed too hard.

"It's a cold day to be out in this weather," he thought. "It's a cold day to die."

Trooper Stuart was coming around a stand of small spruce trees when he saw something ahead. It was the suspect. He couldn't see him clearly, but he could see that he was heading back towards him.

Jeff stopped and backed up a step to hide behind the trees.

"He must have come to the highway and seen the patrol car waiting for him," he thought.

Stuart wanted to radio Jones, but the suspect was too close and he would hear him. He waited with his pistol in his right hand, and with his left hand he pulled his collar away from his body so that he could breathe down inside his parka, hiding his white cloud of breath which might give him away.

Stuart hadn't looked for the cause of Hudson's death. He was so shocked by what he had found that he hadn't thought to look, and now he couldn't remember if there were gunshot or knife wounds. He was mad at himself for not looking when he had the chance, because now he didn't know if the suspect was armed.

The suspect's tracks told him that he wasn't exactly backtracking. He was heading in the trooper's general direction, but not quite to him. Still, he would be within a dozen yards in a minute.

Jeff Stuart crouched and moved carefully to the other side of the tiny island of trees so that he would be closer when the man passed.

From his position, he could see the man clearly. He was very close. He was Indian.

"Five, four, three . . . ," Stuart counted to himself, his whole body tight. He was scared. He didn't like that his partner was back on the road and that he was alone out here.

The Indian was as close as he would ever be to the trees.

" . . . two, one."

Trooper Stuart jumped out from his hiding place, raised his pistol in both hands, and he almost screamed through the night.

"Freeze! Goddamn it. Don't you move! Don't even think about it!" he yelled.

The Indian was caught off guard. He must have known that someone was behind him somewhere, but it was obvious that he still wasn't prepared when the trooper jumped out from nowhere.

The Indian lost his balance and fell.

Stuart ran up until he was only ten feet away from the man, struggling to get up out of the deep snow.

"Don't move," he said.

For the first time Jeff could see the Indian up close. He had long black hair which was tied in a pony tail. He was wearing Hudson's issue parka, and it looked like he had socks on his hands. They were most likely Hudson's too, which made Jeff angrier.

"You're under arrest. If you try to run away, I will shoot you," Jeff said.

From the Indian's expression, Jeff knew that he was understood and that the man knew he was in serious trouble.

Stuart saw a handcuff dangling from the man's wrist.

"I want you to turn towards the highway and walk straight to it," the trooper ordered. He didn't want to attempt to secure his prisoner yet. The hanging handcuff told him that Hudson had already tried. Now he was dead.

The handcuffs reminded Jeff of why he took this job here five years ago. Suddenly, it all came back to him, clear and fresh as the night it happened. He could almost smell the air of the city on that summer night when he and his partner had arrested a rapist, caught in the act in a young widow's bedroom. She had called the police while he was smashing in her bedroom door, and then all that could be heard on the other end of the phone later was her screaming and crying and a man's voice shouting at her to be quiet.

Jeff and his partner arrived late, and the man was almost finished when they finally entered the room, using their flashlights to blind the suspect. The woman's face and hands were bloody and her nightgown was torn. After they finally pulled him off of her and threw him to the floor she ran out of the house screaming.

The man was Hispanic. His pants were below his knees and he wore a dark blue t-shirt. After the rapist pulled up his pants, Stuart's partner felt the suspect's pockets for weapons. He had none. They cuffed his hands together in the front, instead of behind his back, and led him into the livingroom while Jeff went outside to radio dispatch from their patrol car.

Suddenly two shots blasted from inside the house.

A fat orange cat ran out from behind the garage and darted across the street.

Stuart ran into the livingroom and found his partner lying across a wooden coffee table. He had been shot twice, once in the face. Blood poured from his head into a dark irregular pool on the woman's beige carpet. Though Jeff didn't know it at the time, his partner was dead. He ran through the backdoor, through a side gate, and chased the man for five blocks until he lost him on a busy street. Evidently the man had a handgun strapped to his ankle, the one place they had not searched.

When he returned to the crime scene, tired and sweaty, there were other cops already in the house. The widow had returned and she was talking to detectives who tried to calm her. Inside the livingroom he saw the shiny steel handcuffs lying on the floor beside his partner's corpse.

Stuart pushed the vision from his mind and focused on the moment, on this tall Indian who had just killed his friend. Although he couldn't see a weapon, the suspect must have killed Hudson with something. Jeff was taking no chances. He kept the distance between them just far enough, and he made the man place his hands behind his head.

What the officer couldn't have known was that the Indian had no idea where Hudson's handgun was, having tossed it earlier, and that even the knife was lost when the silver cab overturned.

The two men walked onto the road about a hundred yards from the other trooper's dark car. When Jones saw them emerge from the forest, he turned on the car's engine and lights and drove up to where they stood. In his headlights he could see the suspect. The Indian looked nearly frozen to death. He didn't have on a hat, and he was wearing only a pair of summer hiking boots.

Jones stepped out from his vehicle, pulled out his weapon, and ordered the Indian to lie down on the highway. When he did, Jones stood over him with his pistol aimed at the suspect's head while Stuart placed both the man's hands in cuffs behind his back and thoroughly searched for weapons. He checked his ankles twice.

When he was certain that there was no weapons, they led the Indian to the back of the four door patrol car and placed him in the backseat. They closed the door, and both troopers sat up front for the ride down the road to the other vehicles about a half mile or so down the road.

As the car heated inside, Trooper Stuart read the Indian his rights while he tried to warm his hands by rubbing them together. He had removed his gloves as he led the man from the forest so that his fingers would be free to pull the trigger quickly without obstruction if he had to.

On the way, Trooper Jones spoke to Dispatch, telling her that Andy was dead and that they had the suspect in custody.

Within a few minutes, the whole state would know what had happened in that small field someplace in the middle of nowhere. While they waited, the Detachment Commander sent other officers down the road to the scene, and he called to tell the regional Colonel the news.

The three men waited inside the warm car. The moon was covered by clouds again, and it was dark outside. The only light came from the dashboard's soft glow.

Outside, the wind was picking up and they could hear it blowing and feel it mildly shaking the car.

After several minutes of silence, Jeff turned to his partner, looked at him for a long while before he spoke.

"Someone's gonna have to tell Pam," he said.

No one spoke again for a long time.

"Acting like he was the large Porcupine's friend, Raven shot an arrow into a tree stump, and when Porcupine went to pull it out, that black bird shot another arrow right below his armpit where his heart was, killing him."

Chapter 11

The clanging of iron doors startled Highmountain, waking him suddenly. The Indian sat up on a small metal cot and looked around the chamber of the Trooper Station's only jail cell. It took a moment for his eyes to focus. When they did, he saw that he was no longer wearing his own clothes. Instead, he had on a pair of loose-fitting blue pants and a matching shirt and a pair of thin, low-cut canvas sneakers. Then he remembered how he had been brought here through a series of doors, past a couple offices and neat desks.

Philip was the only prisoner. There were no windows or clocks on the walls, and he had no idea how long he had slept, but he knew he didn't feel rested.

The sound that awoke him echoed from down a narrow hallway outside his cell door. The Indian listened to heavy footsteps approaching and then a trooper appeared. The man was short and somewhat overweight and he wore a dark uniform like the cop in the small field of snow and ice. His dark navy pants had a light blue stripe running down the outside of each leg.

The man carried a tray of food. Philip hadn't eaten in a while. He had no idea how long it had been, but the emptiness in his stomach told him that it had been too long. The guard set the tray onto a small ledge in the door and slid it to the prisoner's side, where the Indian grabbed it and sat down on the creaky bed to eat his first meal in what might well have been a day.

The man in the dark navy uniform with the shiny badge watched Philip eat for a minute, then he walked away.

Highmountain was glad for the food, and he was particularly pleased that he had been awakened from his sleep and the dark dreams that came with it. He put his hand to his forehead. It was sweaty and his heart was beating too fast. He felt like he did when he drank too much coffee, the thick stand-a-spoon-in-it kind his grandmother made. They had a word for it in their language: *Guuxi*. They pronounced it "goo-kee."

Philip thought about his dreams. For years he had tried not to think about his brother. They say that some cultures never speak of the dead. Once someone is gone it is as if they never were at all.

Philip remembered an old story from another tribe.

A young man was lost in the forest for a long time and the villagers eventually accepted his death. They held a ritual to cleanse the lost youth's existence from their memory and went on with the business of life. One day, years after the ceremony, the young man returned home. Instead of embracing the lost son, the villagers banished him from the village forever. It seems that you cannot come back from the dead, no matter how strong your pulse.

What happened to James was like that. No one talked about him anymore. It was taboo. What they called in Indian, *engii*.

"And it was too bad," Highmountains thought, "that what happened to him couldn't be shared with young people on the same dark path. They could learn something from his faults, from his death. There was something about life to be passed on from his impatience, from his hurry through the world of the living."

James died in the spring when flowers were opening their soft petals. Grass and trees were turning green, farming nourishment from the soil, their stalks filled, their leafy fingers packed with dirt like old women bent over in vegetable gardens, thinning the rows of weeds.

James had always been a rebel. His whole life was a experiment in failure not always of his own making. When he had a lifetime's worth, he swallowed a bottle of pills which shut his body down, one organ at a time, ending with his kidneys, until he died without announcement and with too few farewells.

Philip was alone with him when it ended. The rest of the family was outside in a waiting room, talking small talk, encouraging each other. Philip had stayed behind. It was a slow way to go, he remembered thinking, not at all like what Kenny had done on his porch with the rifle that other sunny afternoon. Highmountain spent two days in the hospital beside his brother, talking to him when he was both awake and sleeping.

"When you get better," Philip recalled telling his younger brother, pale and yellow-eyed, laying on the hospital bed, "I'll buy you a Harley and we can ride all over together."

James smiled. He always wanted a big bike, but he never had the money to buy one for himself. He had the leather jacket and chained leather wallet, but he never had a ride.

Philip thought James looked very tired. Just the day before things hadn't seemed so bad. James had been sitting up and moving around. He had even eaten his lunch and played a few hands of poker. But the doctor said that it was only a kind of false recovery. She called it Indian Summer and said it was the body's brief respite before its final struggle. Privately, she said that James would die within days. There was nothing to do for him. He died the next day with his brother at his side while the rest of the family sat down the hall drinking coffee and smoking cigarettes and talking about the future and the past.

Now James' jacket hung in the back of Philip's closet

at his mother's house where it had been for almost ten years. Philip had his class ring, too. They were almost all that he had left to remind him of his brother's life.

Philip didn't like to think about his brother's death because he saw too much of himself on that sick bed. James was only two years younger, and their lives were too much alike. Highmountain had always thought how easily it might have been his body that was cremated on that bright spring day.

Philip looked down at the tray. There was only a spoon beside the aluminum plate. He knew from experience he wouldn't be given a fork or knife. The guard was in the outer room and Highmountain could hear him moving around, sliding a chair across the floor.

The Indian stood and walked to the other side of the cell so he could see the guard who was sitting at a small wooden desk. It was an old, military-issue desk, and it had on it a black telephone beside a small radio.

The guard heard Highmountain move and turned around and yelled at him.

"What the fuck are you looking at, goddamn Featherhead? Sit down!" he ordered the prisoner.

Highmountain quickly sat down on the bed and heard the guard switch on the radio. Philip listened to the music while he ate his meal, leaving only a few brussel sprouts on the otherwise empty plate. He had just finished his cup of milk when the news came on. Both men stopped what they were doing and listened to the woman reporter who had a distinct British accent when she spoke.

"Philip Highmountain was arrested late yesterday evening after allegedly and brutally murdering Trooper Andrew Hudson who followed Highmountain into the forest after the Indian's vehicle ran off a highway while being pursued by the trooper."

The guard turned his chair around and faced the prisoner. His eyes were sharp and his jaw was set hard.

"Highmountain, who had been released from prison for the seventh time just the morning before, was suspected of robbing a store at knife point and stabbing Tom Hancock that same day. Hancock is currently listed in critical condition at Crossroads Hospital. Highmountain later stole a taxi and was identified on the highway by Hudson who attempted to arrest the suspect alone. According to reports, Highmountain had a history of violence and alcoholism. Investigators have learned that Trooper Hudson appeared to die of suffocation, although it is not known at this time precisely how he was killed."

The guard placed his right hand against his holster, pulled the black leather strap off with his thumb and rested his palm against the pistol's butt, staring at the Indian, burning his soul with his anger and hatred.

"After a Grand Jury indictment, the District Attorney has told reporters that prosecutors will seek the death penalty for Highmountain."

The last few words echoed in Philip's mind.

Suddenly the guard burst from his seat, grabbed the chair by a leg a hurled it at the cell bars. Philip jumped back, spilling his tray and spoon and brussel sprouts onto the cement floor.

"You're dead, you goddamn bastard!" the guard screamed through the bars. "You're dead. Do you hear me?" He yelled until his face was as red as the fire extinguisher on the wall behind him. Another trooper came into the room and tried to calm the man. They both left a few minutes later, clanging the metal door as it shut behind them.

Highmountain was alone again. The Indian bent over to pick up the mess on the floor and on his bed. When he reached for the spoon on the floor, he saw something beside it. It was a cord. A white parachute cord. It must have been about six feet long.

"It wasn't there before," Philip thought.

He was sure of it. The floor was mopped clean when he came in. Even now he could smell the ammonia from the cleaner.

"It must have been under the plate of food," he said quietly to the emptiness. His echoing voice somehow acknowledged his conclusion.

He picked up the cord. It was thin, but strong, the kind he used moose hunting to hang whole quarters as they cured in the cool fall air. He knew this type came in fifty foot lengths and was strong enough to hold a man's weight.

"But why is it here?" he thought, sitting on the cot, his back against the cold green wall.

Suddenly it came to him.

"They want me to kill myself," he realized. The realization made him shudder.

It was clear. There was no other explanation. Someone had placed the length of cord under his plate. They hadn't given him a knife or fork with his meal, but someone had given him the rope.

Philip jumped up from his cot, flung the cord onto the floor and clutched a steel bar tight in each hand.

"I ain't gonna kill myself!" he screamed at the closed metal door. "I won't!"

He yelled again and again, but no one came. The outside door was shut and he was still alone with the white rope in his cell. He lay down with his face in his hands and his elbows on his knees, and for the first time in years, he began to cry.

He lay there for a long time, looking at the ceiling until he fell asleep. With sleep came dreams. They were relentless and they had pursued him most of his adult life. They waited like thieves and whores in the alleys of his mind until darkness arrived and they could come out unrecognized for what they were.

He saw Mikey picking berries on a clear fall day on the hill behind their village on the river's edge. His son was happy, picking tiny handfuls of blueberries, eating some and dropping others into a coffee can. The can was half full, and Philip could see the boy's purple-stained teeth when he smiled. It was a happy dream. Mikey walked from patch to patch kneeling while he collected the ripe, sweet fruit. The air was fragrant and smelled of berries and fallen leaves.

The boy wandered away from the trail, towards a dark patch of thick alder. Highmountain watched his son as he smiled and waved at his father, his small bucket in his left hand. When Mikey was close to the dense brush, Philip saw the top branches in the middle of the alder patch begin to move. The branches began to sway. Something violent was inside the dark place and moving towards his son.

Highmountain ran as fast as he could, shouting and waving his arms all the while. He ran and ran, but before he could reach the boy, a great bear tore through the dark circle of brush and knocked Mikey to the ground, pinning the boy beneath its weight. There wasn't even enough time for Mikey to scream, but Philip heard screams, loud and long, and he realized they were his own. The bear ripped at soft flesh with long yellow teeth and claws until nothing of the boy remained.

Highmountain hurled himself at the bear, locking one arm tight around its thick neck while he plunged his hunting knife into its side over and over, until the beast's lungs were punctured and it fell dead upon the place were his son had been. Highmountain stood over the bear's carcass and reached down with his right hand to pull out the knife from between its ribs. His left hand was pressed against the animal for support, but his hand felt no fur, only smooth flesh. He looked down and saw that it was no longer a bear, but a man. Philip rolled the corpse onto its side and saw his own face where the bear's short flat face and teeth had been.

The Indian screamed in his sleep. His heart was pounding like it had been before the guard brought in his meal. But he didn't wake up. After a while his body relaxed, his pulse slowed, and he began to dream again.

He was a boy again in his village. Philip was sitting at the small table by the front window of the house he grew up in. Its siding was stained picnic-table red and its tarred roof leaked each spring. Looking out, Philip saw his father teetering down the gravel road, a beer in his left hand. He watched his father stagger towards the house until he vanished at the porch. Highmountain waited, expecting his drunk father to come through the front door any moment. But after a few minutes passed, he stood up and opened the front door, curious what had happened to the man.

His father was on his knees, trying to stand up. Blood, bright as that spring evening, was flowing from his face like the river beyond their driveway. His father had tripped on the first step and fell hard on the porch, too drunk to catch his fall. His face had smashed against the wooden planks and his lip caught on a loose nail which cut his lip clean up to his nose. Blood was splattered all over the steps and all over the front of his white shirt.

Philip pulled off his flannel shirt and pressed it against the wound, trying to slow the blood loss, but his father pushed him away.

"What the hell are you doing, boy?" he asked, his eyes blank.

"You're bleeding, dad." Philip answered. "You fell down."

His father tried to stand up, but he couldn't. Blood gushed all over the ground, pooling on the dirt, slowly seeping into the dry earth.

"I just tripped a little, that's all. I'm alright. Hell, it's just a scratch," his dad continued, looking around for the beer can he had in his hand before he fell.

Philip called for his mother, but she didn't hear him.

"Dad," he said, "you're bleeding really bad."

He tried to hold the wadded shirt against his father's cleft lip, but his dad pushed it away so roughly that it fell out of the boy's hand.

"Shit, kid. Get way from me with that damn thing!" his father yelled, his voice angry and slurred.

Philip knew his dad was drunk. He was drunk most of the time. He knew, too, that his dad was unaware of how badly he was cut or of the volume of blood he was spilling onto the dusty earth which readily drank it in short, fast laps like a dog. He handed the soaked shirt to his father who had managed to stand up, although he was wobbly from the the beer and loss of blood.

"I said get away from me, you little shit!" he yelled as he smacked Philip across the side of his head, knocking him unconscious.

The dream always ended there, although the story went on. He knew that while he lay on the ground in a bright pool of his father's blood, his dad had gone inside and beat his mother for having had a porch built onto the house.

His dad died the next year in a car crash. He was drunk when the car jumped from the highway and plummeted two hundred feet into the lake below, sinking into its sparkling depths like a smooth flat skipping stone.

The first thing Highmountain saw after he opened his eyes was the white cord. It was still where he had left it in a tangled heap a yard from his bed.

Philip had been in jail many times, mostly for violence while drunk. He had even sliced that guy in the bar pretty bad. He was glad, though, that the store clerk was alive. But now he had killed a lawman, and he knew things would be different this time. In his mind he heard the newscaster's voice again.

"Prosecutors will seek the death penalty," the woman reporter had said on the radio.

Highmountain thought about that. No one had ever wanted him dead before. Except maybe his father. He knew things would be different this time. Everyone would hear what he had done. They would all hate him. Sue would hate him even more than she already did, and Mikey would grow up knowing his father was a killer. Everyone would wish that he was dead instead of the trooper.

He wanted to get away from this place, especially now that he was so close to his village and the river. In his mind, he could almost hear the flowing water.

Philip tried to reconstruct the entire struggle in the field, but he couldn't see it. He only saw parts of it. He remembered something from his youth, something about breaking rabbit necks. He knew that it had been dark and that it was very cold outside. He rubbed his hands together, as if warming them. But everything else was gone from his mind. He had no doubt that he killed a man in that field, but he couldn't remember the details.

He ran his hands through his long black hair and his eyes fell upon the cord again. Philip picked it up and studied it. He stretched it out. It was longer than he thought. Maybe eight feet. He pulled it hard. It was strong and smooth and he liked the way it felt. It was the same kind of cord he used hunting to tie off hunks of meat or whole quarters of game onto packboards.

He wound it tightly around his hand and sat back against the wall again, studying the room. There was the small metal cot, a sink, and a rust-stained toilet. The toilet had no seat because it, or the screws holding it, might be used as weapons. The walls were bare and painted a light green. The ceiling was smooth. The iron cell door was black and maybe eight feet tall, going all the way to the ceiling. The door was bolted into the cement floor, on the walls and on the ceiling. There were five bolts on each side. While the thirteen iron bars were vertical and spaced about eight inches apart, there were three horizontal bars that strengthened the entire structure, one at the bottom, one near the middle, and one about four inches from the eight foot ceiling.

Highmountain walked close to the door. The top crossbar was about eighteen inches above his head. He looked up the narrow corridor and listened. There was no sound and no one was coming. He was alone when he unwrapped the white rope, quickly made a loop, and tied a knot, and then, standing with his feet on the bottom crossbar only four or five inches above the floor, tied the other end around the top bar. The noose was just above head level, so Philip pulled himself up the bars, quickly drew the rope over his head with one hand and screamed as loudly as he could.

"Raven called up to Owl from the bottom of the great tree, 'I have some nice straight arrows to give you as a gift.' Raven shot them up towards Owl who kept missing them. 'Lean over a little bit further so you can catch this one,' he said. When Owl leaned over, Raven killed him with the arrow."

Chapter 12

In his own mind, Philip Highmountain was certain that his life was in danger.

He remembered a young hispanic man years ago who died in a California prison after killing a cop. The man was beaten and bleeding when they brought him in to the empty cell beside Philip's. The cops said he got hurt resisting arrest. The inmates knew better, but they had learned not to talk about such things.

The next morning a guard found the inmate dead in his cell. They said that he swallowed his own t-shirt in a suicide, but Philip had heard the prisoner wrestling with some guards in the cell during the restless night before. He knew what happened, and he knew, too, that if he didn't take his own life now, that they might use the rope to take it from him.

That's not the way Philip wanted to die, and he knew that he'd be afraid every time the lock turned in the steel door at the end of the hall.

From his hunting experience, Highmountain knew that the slender, nylon cord would stretch, and he waited until he heard footsteps in the corridor before easing his weight onto the thin white line.

When the guard came in, he saw the prisoner, dressed entirely in light blue clothes, hanging from the steel bar. It was the same trooper who had screamed at Highmountain earlier. The shorter man opened the cell door as fast as he could, and while he stood in front of the Indian trying to figure out how to get Philip down, he noticed something was wrong.

The Indian was normally taller than he was, but Highmountain didn't appear to be as tall as someone hanging a foot or so from the ground. The guard looked down. To his astonishment, he saw that both of the prisoner's feet were firmly planted on the concrete.

He lifted his head quickly to look again at the rope around the man's neck, but just then he was hit hard on the left side of his face, the blow sending him backwards, reeling and tripping on the metal cot against the green cement wall.

Highmountain quickly lifted the cord over his head and jumped onto the trooper before he regained himself from the fall. Before the other man could pull his automatic pistol, the Indian was upon him. They wrestled and the weapon fell to the floor, its clip lying several feet from the gun itself.

The guard yelled for help as loudly as he could. Philip turned and noticed that the metal door was still open slightly. Before someone else came through the door, the Indian kicked his assailant in the stomach, and while the man was bent double, he threw him onto the cot and grabbed the pistol. The clip was too close to the cot, and the man was already trying to get up to reach it. Highmountain knew that the gun was empty, but the other cops wouldn't know it was.

He counted on that much.

He closed the cell door, which slammed noisily, locking the guard inside. Then he ran down the hall and burst into the back room of the Trooper Station, holding the empty pistol in his right hand. An officer who had heard the commotion was coming at him fast.

It was Jeff Stuart. Hudson's friend. The man was close and he was already pulling the thumbstrap off his holster.

Highmountain raised his own weapon with both hands, nervously pointing it at the man.

"Put your hands up or you're dead! Now, dammit!" he yelled. "Now!"

Trooper Stuart, surprised by the escape and caught off guard, took his hand off the holster and put both his hands up.

A woman at a nearby desk screamed and ran out of the room, ducking as if bullets were already flying.

Highmountain was scared and the gun was shaking in his hands.

"Now stand over there," he demanded, nodding his head towards a far wall.

When the trooper was standing by the wall, Philip told him to take off his holster and throw it to him. The Indian tossed Stuart's gun out a window where it landed on the hood of a pickup truck in a shattering of glass.

Then Philip ran through the building and out the front door. The light outside was thick and gray. It was cold, and low clouds were scattered across the horizon. The natural light hurt his eyes and the Indian squinted as he jumped down the stairs of the brown building, taking two and three steps at a time. In the distance, he could see the tops of the eroded cliffs along the river only a mile or so away.

He was almost home.

Highmountain dashed towards the forest across an open parking lot, running towards the river. He could tell by the low sun that it was dusk, and he knew that it would be dark soon. He had to get away from this place while there was still light to see.

The Indian was only a few yards away from the forest edge when he felt a sudden sharp force slam into the back of his left shoulder. The impact made him fall forward, towards the wintering trees, dropping the empty gun as he fell to his knees.

Philip slowly turned his head back towards the building. It was difficult to hold himself up and he had to steady himself twice.

He saw a trooper standing at the top of the stairs with a small pistol between his hands. Jeff Stuart had shot him with a back-up weapon which the officer always carried with him, secured obscurely around his ankle.

Highmountain felt the wound where the bullet exited just below his left shoulder. It was hot and he could see steam rising from his hand when he pulled it back to look at the bright red blood dripping between his fingers and falling onto the fresh powdery snow.

"The great Chief who was tired of Raven's tricks, carried the mischievous bird inside a salmon skin bag high atop a mountain. All the time Raven kept asking what he was going to do. When he reached the peak, the Chief threw the bag with Raven in it over the side. As it fell, it struck jagged rocks and Raven was torn to pieces. The Chief had killed Raven."

Chapter 13

Philip grabbed the empty pistol and rose to his feet, pressing his right hand hard against the wet bullet hole as he staggered into the darkening forest which quickly and efficiently engulfed him, hiding him from the trooper standing at the bottom of the stairs yelling at the Indian to stop running.

Highmountain ran as fast as he could through the deep snow, but then he stopped after about a hundred yards and turned to see if the man who had shot him was following The trees around him were slim and ragged, but there was enough that he could not see the building through them. Philip listened for the sound of someone following, but there was none, only the sound of his own labored breathing and his heart pounding. Behind him was his forced path through the forest and a thin, sporadic trail of blood.

"It would be easy enough to follow me," he thought as he threw the useless pistol into a snowdrift.

In the distance, not too far away, Philip could see the bluffs above the river. He knew his village was nearby and he began to walk towards it. Once again he was ill-prepared for the extreme conditions. In his escape, he had not thought far enough ahead. Now he was once again outside in dangerous weather wearing only the clothes he had been issued while in the cell. He was even less prepared this time. The light blue pants and shirt were too loose and too thin to help him last outside for long.

The temperature was falling as quickly as the setting of the sun. Philip was angry at himself for not planning better.

"None of the plans in my life ever work out right," he thought, stepping over a deadfall half buried in the snow.

"Why should this time be any different?" Highmountain asked himself, especially angry since he had seen a trooper's dark blue parka hanging on a hook on the wall in the building as he ran through it during his rush to escape. He hadn't thought to take it then, and now he had no coat, gloves or hat, and the cheap white tennis shoes he was wearing were entirely useless in the deep snow.

The Indian knew why he wasn't being followed. At first the trooper who shot him could not have known if the pistol Highmountain was carrying was loaded or empty. He would have assumed that it was loaded, and as such, he would have hesitated before pursuing an armed murderer into thick woods where he might be ambushed. There was no reason to pursue him right away, either. It was a clear night and no snowfall was forecasted. The man's tracks would tell them everything they needed to know about his travels, and the blood splatter at the forest edge would tell them that he was wounded. Without proper winter gear and medical attention, they knew that the Indian would not live long.

Philip's feet were frozen. Really frozen. At first the thin white tennis shoes became cold and wet as snow melted into the fabric from his body heat. In no time, however, the wetness became frozen, and then, as he continued to move slowly across the arctic landscape towards the river and an uncertain future, snow packed into the shoes, around and beneath his feet, turning them into blocks of ice. The pain was excruciating at first, but the unbearableness soon disappeared with all feeling. Highmountain knew they were in bad shape, and he stopped once to feel them. They were hard and the flesh around his exposed ankles were discolored.

The bullet wound had stopped bleeding about the same time he had lost feeling in his feet. Only a dull throbbing remained where earlier a stabbing pain had clamped his shoulder tight as a vise.

He could barely move his fingers too, though he ran with both hands under his armpits, and his ears were so cold that Philip imagined they might shatter into pieces if he brushed them too hard against a spruce branch as he ran towards the frozen river.

He had stopped shaking a long time ago.

As the Indian shuffled over a small rise, he could suddenly see lights from a village below. It was his village. He stood on the ridge among trees and wind watching for a long time. A lone raven was squatting on a branch nearby, hunkering close to the tree and sulking as though he were thinking about warmer days. From this high place, Philip could see the feeble light of a snowmobile bouncing as it raced along the wide river's edge towards a neat row of BIA houses which all looked the same.

Highmountain recognized his home and he tried to smile, but his face was too cold to move.

He watched a truck turn from the one main street and pull up beside an old log house. Two people stepped out of the truck and went inside. Smoke from the chimney told him that it was warm.

For a moment Philip thought about the inside of the cabin, and he could almost hear the popping and hissing of wood as it burned in the rattling, black stove's belly, and he could nearly see the picture of the crucified Christ hung on the wall beside a tarnished cross.

The Indian was tired, so he decided to rest before making his way the half mile or so down the hill to the village. He sat with his back against a tree and held his arms close across his chest while he watched the moon rise low above the village. Philip closed his eyes and thought of Sue and Mikey. He thought about his childhood in this place and his many years in prison. He thought of many things until there was nothing left to think and a lasting and dull numbness fell through him like a prayer.

In the quiet of that cold and solitary place, the black bird of Philip Highmountain's spirit floated like a feather above the ancient river of his youth, through the slow burning of winter, into a dark and rolling sundown slowly stealing towards the blue light of a distant, familiar mountain.

This is the first novel by Johnny Saghani (pronounced: Sa-gaw-nee, an Athabaskan word for "Raven"). The son of an Alaska Native father, he was raised in Alaska's interior and along the banks of the Goodpaster River. An avid outdoorsman who enjoys hunting and fishing in the land of his ancestors, he is one of only about eighty speakers of his traditional language and the only one currently writing in it. He lives in Chugiak with his wife, daughter, two cats, and a black lab named Tikaani.